Her breasts rose and fell as she heaved out a heavy breath. "I've made a decision regarding your marriage proposal."

His hand on her arm tightened perceptibly. He'd never expected an answer from her tonight. He'd wanted her to weigh the situation and her feelings about it carefully. But apparently she'd made up her mind without too much thought.

Liam tried to mentally brace himself as he studied her grave expression. "Are you sure, Kitty?"

Her eyes never wavered from his. "Yes. I'm sure that I want to be your wife."

Dear Reader,

As I began to write about the Donovan family, I soon came to the realization that Liam would be the last sibling to find love. It was obvious to me that he was a special man and it would take extra time for the right woman to come along and heal his wounded heart.

Next to love, I believe grief might be the most powerful emotion a human can experience. In some cases it stops a person cold. In others it pushes them to start over and search for a way to fill the emptiness inside them.

In Liam's case, he's lost the will to search for a new beginning, but when he finally does, he slowly realizes that life can offer second chances and love is worth risking everything.

For those of you who've been reading the Donovan stories, thank you so much. And please don't think you have to say goodbye to this family. More Men of the West stories will be coming, and some of them might even include a long-lost Donovan or two!

God bless each trail you ride with love and happiness,

Stella

HIS TEXAS BABY

STELLA BAGWELL

H HARLEQUIN®

entertain, enrich, inspire™

Recycling programs
for this product may
not exist in your area.

ISBN-13: 978-0-373-65681-3

HIS TEXAS BABY

Copyright © 2012 by Stella Bagwell

www.Harlequin.com

Printed in U.S.A.

Books by Stella Bagwell

Harlequin Special Edition

†*Daddy's Double Duty* #2121
†*His Medicine Woman* #2141
†*Christmas with the Mustang Man* #2159
†*His Texas Baby* #2199

Silhouette Special Edition

†*From Here to Texas* #1700
†*Taming a Dark Horse* #1709
†*A South Texas Christmas* #1789
†*The Rancher's Request* #1802
†*The Best Catch in Texas* #1814
†*Having the Cowboy's Baby* #1828
Paging Dr. Right #1843
†*Her Texas Lawman* #1911
†*Hitched to the Horseman* #1923
†*The Christmas She Always Wanted* #1935
†*Cowboy to the Rescue* #1947
A Texan on her Doorstep #1959
†*Lone Star Daddy* #1985
†*Branded with His Baby* #2018
†*The Deputy's Lost and Found* #2039
†*His Texas Wildflower* #2104

Silhouette Books

The Fortunes of Texas
The Heiress and the Sheriff

Maitland Maternity
Just for Christmas

A Bouquet of Babies
*"Baby on Her Doorstep"

Midnight Clear
*"Twins under the Tree"

Going to the Chapel
"The Bride's Big Adventure"

†Men of the West
*Twins on the Doorstep

Other titles by Stella Bagwell
available in ebook format.

STELLA BAGWELL

has written more than seventy novels for Harlequin and Silhouette Books. She credits her loyal readers and hopes her stories have brightened their lives in some small way.

A cowgirl through and through, she loves to watch old Westerns, and has recently learned how to rope a steer. Her days begin and end helping her husband care for a beloved herd of horses on their little ranch located on the south Texas coast. When she's not ropin' and ridin', you'll find her at her desk, creating her next tale of love.

The couple have a son, who is a high school math teacher and athletic coach. Stella loves to hear from readers and invites them to contact her at stellabagwell@gmail.com.

To horses, for the love and inspiration they give us,
and the hopes and dreams we hang upon them.

Chapter One

The woman was pregnant!

Liam Donovan stopped in his tracks and stared down the long shed row. Between him and Kitty Cartwright a hot walker led a sweaty black thoroughbred toward an open doorway, a jockey's valet carrying a saddle and tack hurried past, while a nearby horse hung his head over a gate and nickered loudly. Shafts of sunlight illuminated dust particles and bits of hay dancing through the air, and behind him a worker sang along to a nearby radio. Yet none of those things distracted Liam's focus away from Kitty. Even at a distance, the silhouette of her rounded tummy was very evident and the sight stunned him.

When had this happened? Like a tornado sweeping over the plains, the question roared through his head. Three months ago, when he'd attended her father's funeral in El Paso, she'd appeared as slim as ever. And though they'd only exchanged a few words as he'd offered his condolences, she'd said nothing to even hint at her condition.

But then why would she? The fact that Kitty was having a baby was none of his business. Or was it? He'd only been in her bed that one time. And that had been at least five or six months ago. The bump of her belly didn't look that far along, did it? Besides, if he was the father she would've surely contacted him before now.

As Kitty stood near a stall door, talking with a young man he knew to be an assistant trainer for Desert End, Liam continued to stare. Since he'd only landed in Los Angeles yesterday, Liam hadn't yet learned whether Kitty or the Cartwrights' entourage of horses would be stabled at Hollywood Park Racetrack for the spring/summer meet. He'd heard talk through the racing grapevine that she would be coming, filling the position of head trainer for Desert End Stables; a position that had been held by her father, the late, great Willard Cartwright for forty years. But Liam had tried to ignore the information and tell himself that it didn't matter if or when he might be seeing Kitty again. Now the rapid beat of his heart proved just how much he'd been lying to himself.

Inside the pockets of his jean jacket, his hands curled into loose fists as his gaze took in the lovely tanned oval of her face, the long blond hair spilling down her black sweater, the faded denim hugging her hips and thighs. When he'd first met her seven years ago, she'd been an awkward teenager with a fanatic love for horses. But sometime between then and now, she'd turned into a woman. And now she was carrying a baby. But whose? Could it possibly be his? The question whammed him between the eyes like a sledgehammer driving a steel spike, leaving him feeling dazed and queasy.

"Liam, I'm feeling uneasy about this ankle. I'd like for you to take a look."

The request came from Clint, one of the Diamond D grooms who'd accompanied the Donovan horses to California. Even though the young man was at least ten years younger than Liam's thirty-five, he'd been working for the Donovans since he was twelve years old and since then he'd grown into a competent horseman that Liam could trust implicitly. If he was concerned about a horse's condition, then Liam was concerned, too.

Forcing his eyes away from Kitty, Liam opened the half gate and stepped inside the cinderblock stall, where Clint was standing next to a big red thoroughbred named Reckless Rendezvous.

Normally, nothing distracted Liam from his job. But seeing Kitty again—and pregnant at that—was wrecking his ability to focus. As he knelt next to the right front foot of the horse, Liam tried to clear his mind while he carefully ran his hands over the ankle, fetlock and up the cannon bone. "Nothing feels warm," Liam announced. "And I don't feel anything amiss. Have you noticed any change in his gait?"

Clint said, "Yesterday, when we unloaded him from the plane, I thought he was a bit gimpy. But he could have just been stiff from the long ride. Or it could have just been my imagination. But I'd rather be safe than sorry, so I wanted you to have a look."

Rising to his full height, Liam slapped a comforting hand on the younger man's shoulder. "I don't think there's anything wrong. But we'll get it x-rayed anyway."

"His workout is scheduled for tomorrow morning at seven," Clint reminded him.

"I'll go over to the equine hospital in a few minutes and see about getting the X-ray," Liam promised. "Right now I want to know if you and Andy have settled in and have everything you need."

Clint and Andy, the other groom who had accompanied them on this three-and-half-month stay in California, would be living in small quarters located next to the horses' stalls. The beds were merely adequate and space for more than the bare necessities limited. Liam understood how much the men and his two female hot walkers, who would be housed in another area of the barn, sacrificed in order to do their jobs. That's why the Diamond D paid them handsomely and Liam made sure they had every possible convenience he could give them.

"Sure, Liam. Don't worry about any of us. We're all just excited to be here."

Down through the years, Liam had made a habit of shipping five or six of his better runners to Hollywood Park Racetrack for the spring/summer racing meet. During the three month period, he would fly in and out as each respective race date grew near, while allowing his assistant to remain in California to handle the daily training chores. But Clete, his longtime and very trusted assistant, had passed away a little more than three years ago and Liam still couldn't find it in his heart to even attempt to replace him. The loss had forced Liam to take on more of a workload and change the routine of his plans and schedules.

This year he'd decided to bring his best to the West Coast and personally stay for the entire duration of the meet; unless some unforeseen emergency called him back to the Diamond D. Now, after seeing Kitty in this condition, he wondered if he'd made a huge mistake. Not that he'd come here to have some sort of steady relationship with her. No. They were friends, not lovers. They'd only been together that one time because he'd unexpectedly run into Kitty and her father while visiting Lone Star Park Racetrack in north Texas. The three of them had eaten dinner together, but before the meal was over Will had been called away on business. Liam had remained with Kitty and the two of them had lingered over a bottle of wine. Maybe a little too much wine. Eventually, Liam had offered to walk her back to her Dallas hotel room and once they'd gotten there, one thing had led to another.

Later that night, before he'd left her hotel room, she'd explained that she wasn't ready for any sort of serious relationship with him and that she hoped they could simply go on being friends instead of lovers. Even though Liam hadn't been looking for anything permanent with the woman, his ego had been a bit stung by her attitude. And the idea that she hadn't enjoyed their passionate union enough to want a repeat had been enough to jerk his feet back to solid earth. That same night he'd assured her that nothing had really changed and as far as he was concerned they'd remain friends and nothing more.

The next day he'd flown to Remington Park at Oklahoma City to deal with a runner he'd entered in a Derby and then he'd headed home to New Mexico and done his best to push the woman from his mind. Two months passed without seeing or talking with her. And then the news of Willard's death had stunned the racing world and he'd traveled to El Paso to attend the man's funeral and offer Kitty his condolences.

Since then, he'd continued to fight with the memory of that night they'd recklessly fallen into each other's arms. He'd been telling himself to put it all behind him and move on. She had her life and he had his. And his didn't include having a hot affair with a fellow horse trainer. He wasn't the affair type. Nor was he the marrying type.

And she'd made it clear to him that she wasn't interested in those things, either.

But the memory of making love to Kitty had somehow been burned into his brain and returned to haunt him at moments when he least expected it. And he'd wondered if she ever thought of him and that night, ever longed for him. But now, seeing her belly filled with child, he could only wonder who'd taken his place in her bed. Had she fallen in love? Was she planning to marry?

How do you know some other man has moved into her life? Do you know for certain that the baby isn't yours, Liam? You made love to the woman. And, yeah, she told you she was using birth control, but you're a smart enough guy to know that nothing is one hundred percent effective.

Shutting his ears to the voice going off in his head, Liam dropped his hand from Clint's shoulder and turned his attention back to Reckless. He didn't want to consider that there was a reasonable chance the baby might be his. The idea was too terrifying. He repressed the memories and spoke to Clint.

"If everything checks out okay," he said to the groom, "I want you to have Liv hand walk him in the barn area for about thirty minutes."

"Right. I'll make sure," Clint assured him.

Liam gave him a few more instructions concerning the remaining horses then left the stall in a purposeful stride.

A quick glance to his right revealed that Kitty was still standing in the same area he'd spotted her in a few moments ago. This time she was speaking to a woman who appeared to be a barn worker. Were Kitty's horses also stalled in barn 59? Hell, any other time he would have been happy to share a training barn with the woman. And he'd promised her that they would remain friends. But seeing her pregnant had done something to him. His feelings were being yanked in all different directions.

He was trying to decide whether to go greet her or beat a hasty retreat to his office, when she happened to glance his way. Recognition instantly hit her face and she stared for a few brief seconds before turning her attention back to the barn worker.

If she'd given him a smile, a tiny wave, signaled him with some sort of acknowledgment, he would have gone on to his office and waited for a quieter moment to say hello to her. But her blatant dismissal caught him by surprise and sent him striding down the shed row until he reached her.

"I'll get right on it, Miss Cartwright," the barn worker was saying as Liam walked up to Kitty's left shoulder. "Just let me know if you need anything."

"Thanks, Gina. I appreciate you. Please remember that."

As the tall, huskily built woman turned and hurried away, she nodded a passing greeting to Liam. Once she was out of earshot, Kitty turned and looked up at him.

"Hello, Liam."

Even though there was a faint smile on her soft lips, he could see shadows in her blue eyes and he wondered if grief over losing her father had put them there or something else. Either way, the faint sadness in her gaze didn't diminish her beauty. It struck him hard and jerked him right back to that night when their lips had met and he'd driven himself deep inside her.

"Kitty," he greeted as he tried to stem the erotic memories. "How are you?"

Her smile wavered, but only for a brief moment. "I'm good. Very excited to be back at Hollywood Park. What about yourself?"

She was making an attempt to be cordial, but he couldn't miss the impersonal tone in her voice. He'd not really known what to expect when they met again, away from the crowd of mourners at her father's funeral. In all of his imaginings, it hadn't been like this. Kitty had always been a soft, caring person, a woman who never said a cross word to anything or anyone. With him, she'd always been warm, open and straightforward. He wasn't feeling that now. She was holding back a part of herself and that troubled him. Even hurt him.

"I got here yesterday with the rest of my crew," he told her. "We're just now getting the horses and ourselves settled."

She nodded stiffly. "I wasn't aware until this morning that we'd be sharing the same barn. Did you bring many horses this time?"

"Twenty," he answered. There were eighteen training barns and enough stalls to house nearly two thousand horses on the track, he thought, and somehow he and Kitty had managed to wind up in the same facility. At this moment, Liam couldn't decide whether that was a stroke of misfortune or a piece of good luck.

She looked away from him and swallowed and he used the opportunity to let his gaze slide down to her belly. The soft mound beneath her sweater somehow made her look more feminine and vulnerable and an odd little pang suddenly struck him in the middle of the chest. He wanted to reach out and pull her into his arms so badly he could very nearly taste it.

"Oh. I only brought half that many," she said. "With Dad dying, some of our training got put on hold. A few of the three-year-olds that belong to Desert End still need gate schooling. I may have them shipped out here later for the latter half of the meet."

Desert End Stables, Kitty's home and training facility, was located just north of El Paso, Texas. Liam had visited the place a few times in years past. It was a beautiful horse farm that sprawled for miles over the West Texas desert. Willard had not only been a highly successful trainer, but also a noted breeder in the business. Even though Willard had a son from a former marriage, Liam had heard that Desert End and all its holdings, which would amount to a vast fortune in itself, had gone to Kitty. He supposed the old man had made that decision because Owen had never had anything to do with the horse business and worked as a Deputy Sheriff for Hudspeth County in Texas. Still, Liam had no doubt that Willard had made sure his son had received a fair share of inheritance in monetary form. From all he knew, father and son had gotten along well.

"I miss the hell out of Will," Liam said suddenly, his voice gruff with emotion. "I can't imagine how you must feel."

She looked back at him and he noticed a glaze of moisture in her blue eyes. Maybe he shouldn't have mentioned her father, he thought, but Willard had been a huge presence in both of their lives. His memory could never be ignored or forgotten. It simply wasn't possible.

"Nothing has been easy since we buried Dad," she admitted, her voice low and strained. "But everyone loses a loved one at some time in their life. This time it just happened to be me."

Yeah. He knew all too well what she meant about losing a loved one. One minute he'd had a wife and a baby on the way, the next minute they'd been gone, wiped out of his life when the car she'd been driving through heavy fog had careened off a mountain highway. Since the tragic accident, no woman had caught his interest in any way. Until Kitty. Something about her had made him want again, feel again. And now, with her standing only inches away, she was reminding him that he was a red-blooded man, full of needs and desires.

"I'm sorry, Kitty," he said lowly. "Really sorry."

Her eyes blinked and then she turned her gaze toward the stall to her left, where a black horse was nipping at a hay bag. The nameplate on the stall door read Mr. Marvel and Liam remembered the colt as being one of Willard's favorites. No doubt that everywhere Kitty looked, she was surrounded by bittersweet memories of her father.

Even so, she obviously had other things to think about and plan for, Liam concluded. Like the baby in her womb and the man who'd put it there. Could that man possibly be him? No! It couldn't be. She wouldn't be standing here like this, ignoring the obvious. She would have already told him months ago. Or would she?

Dragging in a heavy breath, he resisted the urge to give his head a shake. This was crazy, he thought. It felt like there was a fire in the barn and both of them were standing there, ignoring it as though nothing was wrong.

Her voice suddenly interrupted his thoughts as she said, "I'll survive, Liam. Dad expected the best from me. I can't break down on him now and ruin everything he worked a lifetime to build."

"Kitty." She sounded so crushed and weary that Liam could hardly bear it and before he could think about it, he placed a comforting hand on her forearm. "Is there anything I can do?"

She didn't answer immediately and Liam supposed his offer didn't mean much. After all, she had the means to hire the best people in the business to keep her stable working efficiently and her win rate at a high percentage. As for emotional support, he figured she had plenty of friends and distant relatives to share her problems with.

She certainly didn't need Liam. The idea left him feeling strangely flat.

"I don't know," she answered finally, then lifted her gaze to his face. "Do you think you could have dinner with me tonight?"

This area of the state was known for its earthquake tremors and for a split second Liam wondered if the ground beneath his feet was tilting. She'd never invited him to join her anywhere, at any time, and he'd always talked himself out of asking her for a date or anything even resembling one. The only reason they'd ever spent time in each other's company was her father. In fact, Willard had once approached him about dating Kitty. The older man had believed that Liam and his daughter would make a fine pair, considering they both loved the same profession. But Liam had dismissed Will's suggestion. At that time his wife's fatal accident had still been fresh in his mind and he'd not been interested in dating anyone. And now—well, he still wasn't interested. Not with the loss of Felicia continuing to haunt him.

He was trying to gather himself enough to respond, when she said, "If you have other engagements don't worry about it. We can get together some other time."

He shook his head as his thoughts raced around her motives and his schedule. "I have to meet someone at seven this evening," he finally said. "But that won't take more than fifteen minutes. Will seven-thirty fit your schedule?"

She looked strangely relieved, a reaction that confused Liam even more. If she'd needed to see or talk with him, all she'd needed to do was pick up the phone and let him know. Her wanting to have dinner with him tonight seemed strange and out of the blue. Yet the idea of spending time with her excited him more than he wanted to admit.

"Seven-thirty would be great," she told him. "You can pick me up at my office. It's at the opposite end of the barn. I've already posted my nameplate, so you shouldn't have any trouble finding it."

"All right. I'll see you then." Realizing he still had hold of her arm, he forced himself to drop his hand. "Is there anyplace special you'd like to eat? I'll make reservations."

"I don't need special. Just anywhere simple and quiet."

"Fine. Seven-thirty then."

A tiny smile lifted the corners of her lips and the sight encouraged him. No matter the situation with this woman's personal life, he wanted her to be happy. Especially with him.

"Yes," she agreed. "Now if you'll excuse me, I have a temperamental mare waiting for me to put on her blinkers."

"Sure," he told her. "I have work waiting, too."

Kitty didn't allow herself a second look at the man as he turned and walked away. She didn't need to. His chiseled features, hazel-green eyes and streaked brown hair were all ingrained in her memory just as much as his tall, solidly built body. He might not be the most handsome guy she'd ever laid eyes on, but he was darn sure the sexiest. And six months ago that latent sexuality had been her undoing.

For days afterward, she'd blamed her reckless behavior on the wine she'd consumed at dinner that night. But deep in her heart she'd known two glasses of wine hadn't made her fall into bed with Liam Donovan.

She'd first met Liam seven years ago, when she'd been nineteen and just beginning to travel extensively with her father. She'd instantly been smitten with the man, not only with his raw, sexy looks, but also with his training skills.

And since that time, little by little, she'd come to learn more about who he was as a man.

Around the track, he had a reputation for being fair and honest, but also hard-driven. Kitty would agree he was all those things and more. He was an extremely private man, who rarely talked about his personal life, which in a way had always made him seem just that much more intriguing to Kitty.

It had been through an offhand comment from her father that she'd learned Liam had lost his wife and unborn child in a car accident a little more than six years ago, but Liam himself had never spoken to her about such things. With her, he'd only discussed training methods, auctions, sires, the pros and cons of different tracks and all the other zillion and one factors that went into racing thoroughbreds. But those discussions had been enough to reveal glimpses of the man and his way of thinking. She admired him, she was wildly attracted to him and she feared she was even in love with him. *Fear* being the key word. Because from what she could see, Liam Donovan was a demanding perfectionist and never would be an easygoing family man. Along with that, her father had admitted, long before he'd died, that he'd tried to talk Liam into dating Kitty and that Liam had refused. If he didn't want to date her, it was a cinch there wasn't a hope in hell that he'd ever fall in love with her.

Oh, God, why didn't she just go home to Desert End and let Clayton take care of things here? There was plenty of work at the farm to keep her more than occupied. A barn filled with up-and-coming two-year-olds, along with a mix of older horses in training for races later in the summer.

But no, she'd chosen to come here. Because she'd known Liam would be here and she'd wanted to see him and be close to him again. Now she had to find the courage to tell him that he was going to be a father.

Swallowing the ball of emotion lodged in her throat, she turned to her left and entered stall number thirty where Blue Snow, one of her prize mares, was housed.

A slight grimace tightened Clayton's features as he looked around at her. "Sorry, Kitty. You'd think by now she would let someone else put these things on her. But the more I tried the more worked up she was getting."

"The last thing I want is for her to get hot and unsettled. So when she acts this way, just let her be and don't worry about it," Kitty instructed her assistant. "The time to start worrying is when she won't let me put them on."

Kitty took the pair of blinkers from him, but instead of rushing at the mare with the piece of equipment, she simply began to stroke her neck and face and talk to her in gentle, soothing tones.

"Is anything wrong, Kitty?"

Not bothering to look at him, she said, "Blue Snow is a bit high-strung. Especially when you're dealing with her head. And I don't have to tell you how important this filly is to me—to Desert End."

"I know all of that. I'm not talking about Snow. I'm talking about you. You look like you've just seen a ghost."

Liam was hardly a ghost. But he'd definitely haunted her thoughts for the past six months, Kitty thought. Ever since she'd gone to bed with him and a baby had been conceived.

"I'm fine, Clayton. I was just hurrying down the shed row and got a little winded, that's all," she explained.

The young man, who'd worked as Willard's main assistant for the past year, cleared his throat. "Well—uh, I noticed you were talking with Liam Donovan. Is he causing you problems?"

Kitty inwardly groaned. Liam had certainly given her a problem, all right. Just not the sort that Clayton thought. But she wasn't about to explain any of this to her assistant. At least, not yet.

Certainly everyone could clearly see she was pregnant. But no one knew who the father was or the circumstances surrounding her condition. And so far her family and friends had respected her privacy and stopped just short of pressing her for the father's identity. She realized that eventually questions would have to be answered; especially to the few family members she had left. But first there was Liam to deal with and she had no idea how he was going to react to her and this news. The mere thought of confronting him left her ill.

"Why would you think he'd be a problem? His horses are stabled on the opposite end of this barn. He'll be coming and going around here just like we will."

The grimace on Clayton's face deepened. "That's exactly why he might be causing a problem. He's damned picky and yells at his hands like they were slaves."

She bit back a sigh. "He wants the best care for his horses and demands they get it. That's all. No one is being forced to work for him."

Clayton snorted. "He has the attitude that his runners are royalty and the rest of us deal in cheap claimers."

Kitty stiffened. She liked Clayton and admired his work even more. She could always depend on him to keep things going whenever she wasn't physically able to keep up. Still, she wasn't going to stand by and let him badmouth Liam.

"That's not true," she said bluntly. "I should know. Liam is an old friend of the family. Weren't you aware?"

The man's face turned red. "Oh. No—I didn't. I mean, I wasn't aware of that."

"He and my father were very close for many years."
She didn't add that she and Liam had been even closer.
Clayton and everyone else would learn that soon enough,
she thought.

"Hmm. That's surprising," he remarked. "I've heard
that Donovan can be a real hard-nosed bastard at times."

"You hear all sorts of things in this business. I wouldn't
put too much stock in it. Success breeds jealousy."

Turning back to the mare, she focused her attention on
slipping the blinkers onto Blue Snow's head. Thankfully
the animal behaved and stood quietly while Kitty adjusted
and buckled the equipment.

"That's true," Clayton agreed. "But frankly, I'm surprised your dad saw that much in the guy. They're two
different types of men."

No, Kitty thought, Liam was very much like her late
father. Maybe that's why she'd gravitated toward the man
in the first place. It was often said that women unconsciously sought out a man with a personality like their
father's. But on the other hand, it was because Liam was
so strong-minded, so driven like Will, that she was now
filled with angst.

When Will and Kitty's mother, Francine, had divorced,
he'd fought fiercely for the custody of his six-year-old
daughter and eventually won. She didn't want to think
that Liam might do the same with this child. She wanted
to believe he was a fair and compassionate man. But this
was an entirely different situation. She wasn't Liam's wife.
Still, with every fiber of her being she longed to be a
hands-on, dedicated mother to her baby.

Deciding she'd already discussed Liam enough with
her assistant, she abruptly changed the subject and did
her best to push the man from her mind.

"Who's scheduled to work Snow this morning? Abby or Rodrigo?"

"Abby."

Kitty said, "Tell her four furlongs, no more. And just because she's wearing blinkers doesn't mean I want her pushed. I only want to see if they'll help keep her mind on her business."

"You going to watch from the stands?"

She glanced at the watch on her wrist. She'd arrived here at the barn this morning shortly before five and it was now nearly eight. By the time she met Liam tonight, she'd be exhausted. But that might be a good thing, she thought dismally. Maybe she'd be so tired she wouldn't care what sort of storm he threw at her.

"I'll be there in five minutes," she told Clayton, then hurried down the shed row to the nearest bathroom.

That evening Liam didn't bother wasting time driving to his summer house to shower and change before he picked up Kitty. In a small office, on his end of the barn, he kept extra clothing and fortunately the bathroom was fitted with a tiny shower, so he made quick use of the facilities before heading down the huge barn to find her.

The day had been an extremely busy one with hardly a moment to draw a good breath. Even so, Kitty had monopolized his thoughts. Asking him to have dinner with her tonight had certainly come out of left field. She'd never made such an overture with him before. True, he'd more or less offered her a shoulder to lean on, but he'd not expected her to take him up on it.

And he could only wonder why she hadn't reached out to him before now. She obviously wanted to talk with him about something, but what? Her father's death and the responsibilities he'd left on her shoulders? The horses in her barn? The baby?

The baby. Ah, yes, he'd thought about the coming child all day, too. About who might be the daddy and what she planned to do once it was born. If he was the father, what would she expect or want from him? Money? Marriage? Nothing? And if he wasn't the father? Well, that notion bothered the hell out of him, too. Making love to the woman that one memorable time didn't give him the right to feel possessive of her or the baby. But he did. And that made him feel like a fool just asking to be hurt.

When he reached her office, he found the door open and Kitty sitting at a desk with a cell phone to her ear.

He made a perfunctory knock on the door facing, then stepped into the space that she'd already put her personal stamp upon with family photos of relatives and friends, along with several significant win photos of various Desert End horses.

The moment she looked up and spotted him standing just inside the door, she abruptly ended the conversation and lowered the phone from her ear.

"I hope I didn't interrupt something important," he said.

A faint smile touched her face and Liam was struck by the shadows of fatigue smudged beneath her eyes, the faint droop to her shoulders. A racehorse trainer put in long, arduous hours of work. It was tiring even for a strong, healthy man like himself. He couldn't imagine what it must be doing to Kitty in her delicate condition. The mere thought of anything happening to her, or the child, made him inwardly shudder and he suddenly realized how very much he wanted to protect them both.

"An owner," she explained. "You know how it is. Sometimes they worry over nothing and call five or six times a day. That was the third call today for this particular owner."

She rose to her feet and he could see that she'd changed into a dove-gray dress that draped modestly over her growing belly. The hem struck her midcalf and brushed against a pair of black dress riding boots. Her blond hair was twisted into a knot at the back of her head and secured with a tortoiseshell clip. In spite of her obvious fatigue, she looked beautiful, even more beautiful than he remembered throughout the long winter months they'd been apart.

"Unfortunately coddling owners is a part of the job," he replied.

She plucked up a black handbag from the corner of the desk and joined him at the door. "I'm ready if you are."

"You might need a jacket," he suggested. "Even though it's the beginning of April it feels more like February out there. The evening has already turned very cool."

After eyeing the heavy fabric of his shirt, she walked over to a tiny closet and pulled out a red woolen cape. Liam quickly moved to help her place it around her shoulders. As he smoothed the fabric against her back, he noticed that she smelled like some sort of sweet flower and just being close to her shook his senses.

"I made reservations at a seafood place," he told her as he pushed her hands out of the way and fastened the silk frog at her throat. His fingers inadvertently touched her chin and the softness of her skin left him wanting to touch more. "I remembered that you like shrimp scampi."

She looked up at him and suddenly her lips were quivering, her eyes misting over. "The last time we had dinner together Dad was with us. He was always with us, wasn't he? And now— Oh, Liam, help me," she whispered brokenly.

Raw emotion struck him in the middle of the chest and all he could do was gather her into his arms and pull her tight against him.

For long moments, he held her quietly, until she finally sniffed and tilted her head back far enough to look up at him.

"I'm so sorry, Liam. I'm—" With a tortured groan, she pulled out of his embrace and turned her back to him. "I'm sorry I'm pulling you into my misery. And I—"

He was fighting the urge to reach for her again when she whirled back to him. This time her features were twisted with agony. "I'm sorry that I have to tell you that you're going to be a father."

Chapter Two

Liam stared at her as his thoughts whirled at a mind-numbing speed. "Me? You're saying I'm the father of your baby?"

Pressing a palm against her forehead, she closed her eyes. "I shouldn't have blurted it out like that. I hadn't planned to. I wanted to wait until after we'd had dinner and…" She opened her eyes and slowly, guardedly searched his face. "What are you thinking?"

He swallowed as he tried to gather his thoughts and form some sort of coherent answer. All day long he'd been telling himself that the likelihood of the baby being his was practically nil. He'd tried to convince himself that after their one-night fling, she'd moved on to someone else, some man that had become a permanent fixture in her life. Yet deep in his gut he'd sensed that she was carrying his child. Now that she'd spoken the fact aloud an odd mixture of emotions was rushing through him, filling him with fear and euphoria.

"I'm thinking—"

His words were interrupted by the sound of footsteps directly behind him, and then a knock on the door.

"Hey, Kitty, you gonna need me tomorrow?"

Glancing over his shoulder, Liam saw Rodrigo, one of the exercise riders that Willard had used for the past few years. The young man was grinning as though he didn't have a care in the world. And Liam suddenly wondered how it would feel to live each day without a heavy weight of responsibility on his shoulders. But from the time he'd been a very young man in high school, his father had pinned high expectations on him. Ones that Liam was still striving to meet.

Clearing her throat, Kitty said, "I need three ridden in the morning, Rodrigo. Get with Clay. He should still be here in the barn. If not—" She quickly scribbled a phone number on a scrap of paper and carried it over to the jockey. "Call him and he'll give you the time schedule and instructions."

Rodrigo thrust out his hand and gave Kitty's an enthusiastic pump. "Thank you, Kitty. Thank you very much. See in you in the morning, then. Okay?"

Kitty gave him a genuine smile. "I'll be here," she promised.

The jockey quickly trotted off and Kitty slowly turned back to Liam.

"I think we should—" The ring of a cell phone inside her purse interrupted her in midsentence. Casting him a rueful glance, she fished out the instrument. "Sorry, Liam. Let me turn this off."

He waited while she dealt with the phone then quickly

took hold of her upper arm. "Let's get out of here," he muttered, "before someone else comes along."

They left the office and walked outside to a parking area used by barn workers, trainers and their employees. Without exchanging any words, Liam helped her into the bucket seat of his plush truck.

It wasn't until he'd driven away from the racetrack and turned onto the freeway that he felt composed enough to speak.

"I don't understand this, Kitty. We were together six months ago! Why didn't you—"

Her expression imploring, she looked at him. "Let's not discuss this while we're traveling down the freeway, Liam. I think the issue deserves more attention than that," she said.

He suddenly realized his hands had a choke hold on the steering wheel and his breaths were coming short and fast. He had to get a grip and face this situation with sensibility, he thought. Losing his cool now would be pointless, along with making him look like a complete ass. A baby did deserve his complete attention. "All right," he agreed. "We'll talk over dinner."

Thankfully, the restaurant Liam had chosen wasn't that far from the track. In less than fifteen minutes they were inside the small eating place, seated near a window overlooking a courtyard. Darkness had fallen over the city, but foot lamps illuminated a small garden area landscaped with palms and flowering shrubs.

After the waiter left to attend to their orders, Kitty silently stared out the window. As Liam studied the lovely lines of her face, he decided the gray, gloomy weather that had moved in earlier this afternoon matched the sadness in her eyes.

Was that sadness stemming from the loss of her father

or the fact that she was unexpectedly having a baby? His baby! Liam didn't think he'd yet fully comprehended the news she'd just handed him. Yesterday he'd been a widower with nothing more than horses on his mind. Today he was going to be a father!

The idea had put his emotions on a roller-coaster ride. What if something tragic happened to her or their baby? What if something happened to rip his son or daughter away before he ever had the chance to be a father to the child, the same way it had happened seven years ago? Yet even as these fearful questions were rushing through his head, he wanted to shout with pure joy.

"I realize it's hard for you to understand why I've not said anything to you about the baby before now," she said suddenly. "But I'm not going to apologize. It wasn't until after Dad died that I learned for sure that I was pregnant. And at that time I had other pressing things to deal with."

Becoming a parent was a pressing thing. Or didn't she think so? Liam wondered. He wanted to fling the question at her, but stopped himself short. Losing her father had undoubtedly turned her world upside down and now she had her pregnancy to deal with. She deserved some slack, not upbraiding. Especially from him.

Glancing around, he noticed that he and Kitty were the only two people sitting in the small alcove. The quiet coziness reminded Liam that, except for that one night they'd shared a bed, they'd hardly ever spent time alone together. And yet they were having a baby. He'd have bet the chances of that happening were less than Liam winning the Kentucky Derby.

"You've had one shock follow another," he pointed out.

Her blue eyes were tinged with regret as they scanned his face. "Yes. And now I've given you one." Sighing, she shook her head slightly. "Dad's heart attack came without warning. He was always so strong and healthy. And then suddenly he was gone and my brother was away and I was faced with making funeral arrangements, watching my father being lowered into the ground and then trying to decide if I could go on with the horses. Not just Desert End horses, but those of our clients'. Without Dad, my whole world was turned upside down and I wasn't sure I could handle the responsibility of running the farm or handling the finances. And then I found out about the baby and I wasn't even sure I could handle being a mother."

Her last words caused Liam to freeze inside. To think that she might have considered terminating the pregnancy chilled him to the bone. He'd already lost one child as it grew in its mother's womb. To imagine losing a second baby was completely terrifying. He didn't have to ponder; he already knew he wanted this child. Very much. "You mean—you considered not having the baby?"

The disbelief in his voice must have conveyed his painful thoughts because she grimaced, then once again shook her head.

"I've always known I would go through with this pregnancy, if that's what you mean. But I—" Her gaze suddenly dropped to her lap. "Well, everything fell on me at once. It's taken a while for me to come to grips and make a plan for my future—a future without Dad at my side."

She'd had more thrown at her in a matter of days than some people had in a lifetime. Liam could understand her emotions had been thrown in upheaval. And he wasn't here to vex her with more problems. But he did deserve answers about the baby. *His* baby! The reality of it continued to stun him. Since he'd lost Felicia and the baby, he'd never been able to muster any serious interest in another woman. As a result, he'd practically given up on having

a family of his own. Now, in the blink of an eye, all of
that had changed.

He cleared his throat, but his voice came out little more
than a hoarse whisper as he spoke. "I'm grateful, Kitty,
that you didn't want to end the pregnancy."

Her blue eyes flickered with something like relief and
the sight surprised Liam. Had she expected him to be
angry about her pregnancy? Or, God forbid, not want the
baby? He might come across as a real bastard at times, but
that was only when he was dealing with inept or uncaring
stable hands. Not with the people he loved.

But he didn't love Kitty. No. He didn't even know her
enough to love her. He liked and admired her. And he was
damned attracted to her. But that was a long way from
love. Besides, all of his love, his whole heart, had been
buried with his wife and child. He didn't have any left to
give this woman.

"You mean you're not upset about this?" she asked.

Liam had to admit his emotions were running the full
gamut right now. Shock, fear, joy and amazement were all
tumbling through him, but he could safely say that anger
was not among those feelings. How could he be resentful when a child was something he'd once longed for and
dreamed about?

Solemnly, he reached across the table and enfolded her
hand in his. "Why would I be?"

A dark pink blush swept up her neck and over her face.

"Because that night I assured you everything was okay.
And I believed it was. But the protection I was wearing
slipped from where it was supposed to be. The doctor assured me that there was only a tiny chance of that ever
happening. I guess a tiny chance was working against us
that night."

"Or for us," he added. "Depending on the way you look at things."

He was going to have a child! He was going to be a father! With each passing minute the realization was slowly and surely sinking in on him and he was amazed at how comfortable he felt with the idea. Especially when he'd spent the past six years of his life convincing himself that it wasn't meant for him to have a family.

A wan smile touched Kitty's lips. "I'm glad you're not upset. Some guys wouldn't be so—understanding."

"I'm not *some* guy," he said with distaste, then leveled a pointed look at her. "But to be honest when I first saw you this morning and noticed that you were pregnant, I figured you'd met a man and were on your way to becoming a wife."

Her lips parted to speak just as the waiter arrived with a cocktail for Liam and a ginger ale for Kitty. After the young man had served the drinks and walked away, she gave him a halfhearted smile. "When would I have time for a man?"

Her comment caused his brows to lift slightly. She might not have spent much intimate time with Liam, but she'd definitely made their evening together count. "You had time for me."

Curling both hands around her glass, her smile faded as she stared down at the bubbling liquid. "You and I both know that we suffered a lapse of sanity that night. We might be having a child together but we're not a couple. We never have been."

Even though every word she'd uttered was the truth, Liam didn't like the way it sounded. So indifferent and casual, so uncaring. He wasn't in love with Kitty but he did care about her. Very much. Yet he wasn't at all sure that she reciprocated his feelings. And that made him feel like a teenager with a hopeless crush. If the situation wasn't so serious it would almost be laughable. The only females Liam ever mooned over were fillies or mares with the potential to win a six-figure purse. It shouldn't matter to him if Kitty held any sort of affection for him.

"I guess not," he agreed. "But the baby has connected us. It will keep us connected for the rest of our lives."

She sipped her drink then glanced awkwardly away from him. "Yes. I suppose you're right about that."

He swiped a hand through his hair, rumpling the rich brown waves. "Me, a father," he said with dismay. "I've got to admit I'd already moved past the notion of having a child in my life. I had decided I wasn't ever going to be a father."

She studied him thoughtfully. "You're still a young man, Liam. It's hard to imagine you already writing off those aspects of your life."

He blew out a heavy breath. "Can't you? I'm sure Will told you about…well, about my family and…what happened."

Even now, in spite of his efforts to move forward, speaking about Felicia and the baby was like staring into a dark, empty hole. His family had oftentimes accused him of trying to cling to a memory and hang uselessly on to the past. But that wasn't quite the truth. He'd tried to forget and set his sights on the future. He'd thrown himself into his work and pushed himself to get interested in dating and women. The work had helped keep his mind occupied, but he'd never felt a flicker of attraction toward another woman. Not until Kitty. And even that had been a slow thing that had crept up on him before he'd realized it was even happening. Now that attraction had turned into a baby!

He watched her cloudy gaze drop to the tabletop. "Yes.

Dad told me a few years ago about the accident. I never mentioned it to you before because—" She focused her eyes back on his face. "Well, that's your private business. If you wanted to talk to me about it that was for you to decide. Not me."

"I rarely talk about it to anyone."

Her expression solemn, she asked, "So the accident is why you never planned to have a family again?"

"My family was taken from me. I knew I couldn't replace them." He shrugged even though he was feeling anything but casual. "Felicia was one of a kind. She understood me and I understood her. We always got along without a hitch and the baby was a dream come true for the both of us. Once they were gone there was nothing left in my life but an empty hole. And I've never seen any way to fill it."

"I see," she murmured stiffly.

Did she? Most of the time, Liam had difficulty understanding his own feelings about the situation so he doubted she could grasp the state of his heart. But whether she appreciated how that part of his past had affected him didn't really matter now. This was a new baby. And even though he'd not planned on it, his life was about to change.

"That probably sounds hard to you. If it does, I'm sorry. I'm not really a hard man, Kitty."

A faint smile touched her lips and Liam was surprised at how much he would like to kiss her, to have that soft sweetness against his mouth, feel her warm breath caress his cheek.

"I've not ever thought that about you, Liam. Driven maybe. But not hard."

He took another sip of his drink and realized the cocktail wasn't nearly strong enough to slow the whirling thoughts in his head. Normally he was a cool, calculating man, his mind razor sharp. But Kitty and news of the baby had melted the ice water in his veins. Damn it. Right now he was feeling too much. Thinking too much.

"My work is what keeps me going," he admitted. "Ever since I lost Felicia and the baby I've made horses and racing my whole life."

"Well, you're definitely making a name for yourself. For the past few years you've made plenty of owners and trainers bow down to you."

He chuckled at her choice of words. "Bow? I didn't know anyone had ever seen me wearing my crown, I always make a point to leave it locked in the vault at home."

The smile fighting its way across her face warmed him.

"You hardly need to wear a crown, Liam. Everyone around the West Coast tracks think you're royalty."

"Only the West Coast?"

That made her laugh and he realized it was the first joyous sound he'd heard her make today. He also realized how good her laughter made him feel.

"I don't know why anyone would have that idea about me," he said with a shake of his head. "I've never won a training title at any track in this area. Up until this year I've never brought that many horses to California to even vie for one."

"No. But you have a high win percentage with the amount you do bring," she pointed out.

The waiter arrived with their salads and once they were alone again, she wasted no time in drenching the pile of greens with black pepper and forking up a piece of romaine lettuce.

Following her example, he dug into his own salad and swallowed several bites before he spoke again. "I've brought some of my best out here this spring. I'm hoping to show some of the big owners and trainers that the Diamond D stables can compete on any level."

She sighed. "I'm hoping just to measure up to Dad's standards. And that isn't going to be easy."

"Nothing about this business is easy." He settled a soft gaze on her face. "But you shouldn't worry, Kitty. You'll do your father proud."

Kitty looked at him and was suddenly horrified to feel tears glazing her eyes. All day long she'd promised herself that she wouldn't become emotional tonight while she sat across the dinner table from Liam. But that promise had been impossible to keep. When he spoke of her father it ripped her heart. And when he'd talked about losing his wife and baby, she'd felt deep down hurt. For him and for herself. It was clear to her that he was still suffering and that meant he wasn't ready to love again. Not her or any woman. Oh, God, why did that crush her so? Why couldn't she look at him, be near him and feel nothing more than mild affection?

"Well, I'm going to do everything in my power to make him proud," she said huskily. And to hold on to what was rightfully hers, she could have added. But tonight wasn't the time to tell Liam about the edict her father had left in his will. Tonight was about the baby and how the two of them were going to deal with becoming parents.

A faint smile touched his lips and Kitty felt her heart flutter like a young girl experiencing her first crush. It was crazy to be reacting to this man in such a way, yet at the same time it was exhilarating. And she suddenly realized that Liam had done something she'd thought impossible. He'd broken through the numbness of her grief and made her feel again, want to live again.

"I have no doubts about that," he said. "The first time I ever met your father, you were trailing alongside him.

I'm sure during all those years you've absorbed a wealth of knowledge."

She certainly had, Kitty thought dourly. She'd learned firsthand knowledge about controlling men and fractious horses. Neither of which she'd learned how to handle entirely.

"I tried," was all she allowed herself to say.

He ate several bites of salad then said, "So tell me about your health. Are you feeling well? And the baby?"

Glad that he'd given her a couple of easy questions, she nodded. "I had a few bouts of nausea in my second and third month. But that's past. So far I'm doing fine. And the baby appears to be healthy and growing."

He looked visibly relieved and she could only wonder what the news of this baby had done to him. Brought up memories too painful to bear? Or was he seeing this child as a second chance for him to be a father? If they were a true couple she wouldn't be wondering about those things, she would already know. But Kitty doubted they would ever be that close. Close enough for her to see into his heart. The notion saddened her. She'd always wanted to be important to this man and now that she was having his child that need had only intensified.

"I'm glad. Let's pray everything stays that way," he said then asked, "When are you due to give birth?"

Yes, he would be praying, she thought. She could already see that he wanted this child and since he'd already lost one baby, he probably wouldn't relax until this one had safely arrived. And no doubt the loss of that earlier child would only make him want to cling to this one even more.

It terrified her to think he might eventually want to yank their child from her arms and carry it back to his home in New Mexico. As Clayton had hinted, Liam could be ruthless toward his staff if he believed they were neglecting their duties. She didn't want that merciless determination directed at her or their child. But so far tonight, she'd not picked up on any sign of that, thank God. Because she had no intention of giving up her rights as a mother.

"The first week of July or somewhere near then," she answered then sighed with resignation. The American Oaks would be running almost at the same time. It was the race that would determine the very fate of her career. She had to win, or at the very least place in the top three. Otherwise, she was in danger of losing everything.

"That's right in the heart of racing season."

"You don't have to remind me. I have Black Dahlia's nomination fee for the Oaks already paid. I'll probably go into labor when the bugler calls for post time," she said with wry humor. "But we'll see. Whatever happens, Clayton is a very good assistant. I can trust him to handle things while I'm in the hospital."

She could feel his gaze sliding keenly over her face and she fought the urge to shift uncomfortably in her chair.

"And afterward?" he asked. "What do you plan to do then?"

She tried to swallow another bite of salad but her throat seemed to clamp around the chewed food. "I'll go home to Desert End for a couple of weeks to recuperate and then I'll head back to the track with baby and a nanny in tow."

His face showed little to no expression as he looked at her. "So you don't plan on quitting your job as a trainer."

She did her best not to bristle. The man had to ask questions. He couldn't read her mind in order to know her plans for the future. Still, his remark was a bit sexist and if anyone else but him had asked it, she wouldn't waste her breath giving them an answer.

"Not hardly. Do you?"

As she watched a deep red blush crawl up his throat, she could see he was annoyed, embarrassed or both.

"Sorry. That wasn't a good question to ask."

"Think about it, Liam. I can be a mother and a trainer at the same time. Just like, I hope, you can be a father and a trainer at the same time." She leaned earnestly forward. "I hardly intend to shove my baby aside and let someone else do the hands-on care. I intend to love and nurture it just as any mother would do. But no matter which one of us is physically caring for the child, we'll have to have a nanny's help."

He reached for his water glass. "I understand that. I— Well, clearly you weren't expecting a child to enter your life at this stage and neither was I. But that doesn't mean we don't want the best for this baby."

She nodded. "I totally agree."

"What about Will—did he know about the baby before he died?"

Regret settled on Kitty's shoulders and she looked at her half-eaten salad rather than meet his probing gaze. "No. A few weeks before his death I wasn't feeling well. But my cycles have always been irregular, so pregnancy never really crossed my mind. I thought I had some sort of stomach issue caused by stress. By the time I saw the doctor Dad had the heart attack and then it was too late."

"Hmm. I wonder what he would have thought about the baby."

She rubbed fingers against the tiny throb behind her forehead. Her father had adored Liam. No doubt he would have been thrilled about the baby. "I think about that a lot, Liam. And you can't imagine how much I wished he'd known. He— Well, he might have been disappointed that I was bearing a child out of wedlock, but I feel sure he would've been excited to be getting a grandchild. He'd pretty much given up on Owen giving him any. And he figured if I had to choose between a man or a horse, I'd always choose the latter."

The grimace on Liam's face had Kitty studying him more closely and what she saw fairly took her breath. He'd always been a striking figure of a man, but it seemed as though the past year he'd become even more attractive. Maybe that was because he'd let his hair grow down on his collar, or because he sometimes avoided shaving and the dark brown stubble on his face added to his rough-hewn features. His clothes, at least at Hollywood Park, had become more casual, too. Most of the time, he was dressed in blue jeans, boots and a Levi's jacket.

Liam Donovan might be considered royalty, but he wasn't one of those trainers that went around in a suit and tie with every hair in place and did all of his work over the phone. No, he was a hands-on type of guy who wasn't afraid to get dirty and often did.

"I don't expect he would have been very proud of me," he said with a measure of self-contempt. "He was a mentor and I feel as though I let him down."

His remark had her looking at him with dismay. "You let him down? How do you think I feel? He was my *father*. I did let him down. In more ways than one."

He didn't press her to explain that comment and Kitty was glad. She didn't want to explain how she'd let her father down by refusing to marry Steve Bowers or how she'd embarrassed him by throwing Roger Grove's engagement ring back in his face. Over the years, her father had held his own ideas about who she should love and marry and she'd disappointed him by rebelling, by questioning his judgment. But try as she might, neither of those men had been the sort she'd envisioned spending the rest of her life with. As a result, she'd ended both relationships. It was ironic, she supposed, that the only time her father had picked out the right man for her, Liam had refused.

She'd never told Liam that she'd learned of her father's effort to get him to date her. And she wasn't about to reveal it to him now. It was all too humiliating. Especially now that she was carrying his child.

Trying to shove those miserable thoughts away, she looked around with relief to see the waiter arriving with their main courses. She needed to eat and escape to her hotel room where she could go to bed and hope the weariness in her body and soul would disappear, at least for a while.

After the waiter had left behind Kitty's shrimp scampi and Liam's stuffed crab, he said, "Will understood human nature. He didn't expect people or his horses to be perfect."

She picked up her fork. "Dad expected it of me."

Disbelief appeared on his face in the form of a frown. "I never noticed that whenever I was around the two of you."

She sighed. Willard Cartwright had been a likable guy with a warm, jovial personality. He'd made friends easily and she doubted he'd died having even one enemy. Unless she counted her mother, Francine. As Willard's wife, she'd refused to allow him to dominate every aspect of her life and because of that they'd gone through a bitter divorce and an even nastier custody battle over Kitty. With his family members, Willard had been a different man, one who'd loved fiercely, but had also fought to be in control. Now he was still trying to control Kitty from the grave.

She said, "Families always behave differently at home than in public."

"That's true," he agreed. "But I always got the impression that you adored your father."

"I did adore him. He was wonderful to me and Owen

in so many ways. But he was demanding and controlling and because of that we often clashed—sometimes very loudly." A bittersweet smile suddenly touched her lips. "Still, he was bigger than life and I wanted to be just like him. At least, like the good parts," she amended. "Now— well, now I just miss him like hell."

"If I lost my father, I'd be devastated," he said solemnly.

Kitty had met Liam's parents, Doyle and Fiona, about two years ago at Sunland Park near El Paso. They'd had a colt running in the Sunland Derby and most of the Donovan family had traveled to West Texas to view the event. Fiona had been breathtakingly beautiful, classy and very approachable. In looks, Doyle had been an older version of Liam, but the elder Donovan had seemed to be a genuinely happy and jovial man, whereas Liam was usually serious and all business. She'd liked his parents and his family. In fact, she'd been envious of their close-knit bond.

"So how are your parents doing? Do they plan to come out to Hollywood anytime during the meet?"

"They're doing great. And as of now they're planning on coming for the Big Cap and maybe, later on, the Gold Cup. It depends on what's going on with their schedule. They say they're retired, but they're busier now than they've ever been."

Feeling suddenly pensive, she pushed the food around on her plate. "You were just wondering what my father would have thought of our situation. Now I'm wondering what your family is going to think?"

"Does it matter?"

Her gaze lifted from her plate to settle on his face. "I suppose it shouldn't. We're not teenagers. We're grown adults, financially secure and settled in our careers. If we're not capable of raising a child, then I don't know who would be. But…" Looking away from him, she released a wistful sigh. "I've got to be honest, Liam. Their opinion of me does matter. After all, this will be their grandchild."

He reached across the table and touched his fingers to hers. The simple gesture sent a wave of emotions rushing through her. She blinked and swallowed and prayed she could keep her tears in check.

"Believe me, Kitty, my parents will welcome you into the family with open arms."

A confused frown pulled her brows together. "You mean they'll welcome the baby with open arms," she corrected. "He or she will be a part of the Donovan family. Not me."

A faint smile lifted one corner of his mouth. "The baby is already a Donovan. And so will you be—just as soon as you become my wife."

Chapter Three

The grip she had on the fork loosened and the utensil fell with a loud clatter to her plate as she stared at him in stunned fascination.

"Your wife!" she gasped. "Are you serious?"

A frown furrowed deep lines in his forehead. "You didn't expect anything less of me, did you?"

Amazed that he was suggesting such a commitment between them, she said, "I expected you to see this whole situation in a sensible way. I didn't think you'd have this old-fashioned view that a woman expects or wants the father of her child to marry her!"

He leaned back in his chair and fixed her with a meaningful look. "And I expected you to want to do what's right and best for our child."

She swallowed as questions and thoughts barreled through her mind. "And you believe that the two of us getting married is the right and best thing?" she asked, her low voice full of dismay.

"Come on, Kitty, surely it crossed your mind that I would suggest marriage."

Actually, the idea had crossed her mind a time or two, but she'd instantly pushed it aside. Everyone knew that Liam wasn't the marrying type. He'd even told her father as much. And he didn't want to marry now. Not really. This was all for the child and no other reason.

"To be honest, the idea did cross my mind, but it passed too quickly to ponder. Everyone, including me, knows that you're a confirmed bachelor."

"Wrong. I'm a widower. A widower who'd never planned to marry again."

She looked away from him and tried to stem the sick feeling swimming in her stomach and spreading up to her chest. Did he have any idea how that statement made her feel? He might as well have come out and bluntly stated the facts. The night they'd made love, he'd never thought about a future with her. She'd suspected it, but hadn't wanted to admit it.

You knew that when you invited him into your bed, Kitty. Just because he's saying it out loud and to your face doesn't make it any more hurtful. So get over it.

"And I'm a single woman, who intends to stay that way—at least, until the baby gets a bit older."

"Why?"

Jerking her gaze back to his face, she stared wondrously at him. "Because I..." Her voice trailed off as she tried to gather the right words, the best explanation she could possibly give without revealing too much of herself. "Okay, I'll try to explain, Liam. When most women, including myself, dream of getting married it's all about romance and love. Convenience or practicality doesn't figure into things. If I can't have the sort of marriage I want, I'd rather stay single."

He shoved out a heavy breath as he carefully placed his fork next to his plate. Apparently, he'd lost his appetite, too, she thought sickly.

"I wish things were different, Kitty. For you and for me. But I'm fairly certain that you're not a selfish woman. At least, I've never seen that side of you before. And once you think about this, you'll realize that our baby takes priority over our own wants and needs."

Tears were beginning to burn the back of her eyes and the hunger that had been gnawing earlier at her stomach had now completely vanished. He was right in so many ways. But that didn't lessen the loss of her dreams and all that she'd ever hoped to have in her life. He was a practical man, not a romantic like her. He was viewing this whole issue with his head, while she was seeing it through her heart.

"I understand that we need to put the baby's welfare first, Liam. Right now I just don't see a marriage between us making anything better for this coming child."

Grimacing, he reached for his cocktail glass and drained the last of its contents. "A child needs two parents," he said as he placed the empty glass aside. "Parents who live together."

Not like the Cartwrights, who'd divorced, then fought over their child in a cold courtroom, she thought. From the time Kitty had reached the age of six, she'd lived without a mother. Clearly, Liam was aware that her parents were divorced, but whether he knew she'd been raised solely by her father through all those tender years, she couldn't say. She'd certainly never discussed such a personal matter with him. But for all she knew, her father could have confided in him.

"I guess you would know more about that than me. You have a big, united family," she said quietly. "My parents divorced when I was six. And after that my mother was no longer a part of my life."

A rueful grimace tightened his features. "I'm sorry, Kitty. Will said something to me once about his ex not being much of a mother. But I didn't ask him to explain the remark. I don't like people prying into my private life, so I respected your father's privacy and kept the question to myself."

She shook her head. "There's not really much to explain. After my parents divorced Dad won custody of me. Francine went back to Georgia where she was from originally and began another life—without her daughter."

He studied her face for long moments and Kitty hated the fact that tears were doing their best to form at the back of her eyes. Normally, she could speak about her mother without getting emotional. Over the years, she'd told herself it didn't matter that her mother had practically forgotten she'd had a daughter. But being pregnant had left her soft and vulnerable, had left her wondering how any mother could simply walk away from her child.

"I see. Well, that ought to make you better understand how a child needs both parents—together," he said finally.

Her stomach was tying itself into painful knots. "I agree that two parents in a loving home is the ideal setup for a child's upbringing. But that's not us. We're friends. Who—well, just happened to have sex one night."

She hoped she'd sounded as cool and practical as when he'd talked about never planning to marry again. Not for anything did she want him to know how besotted she was with him and had been for some time now.

He let out a long breath. "That's true. And now we

need to deal with an unexpected situation—in the best way possible."

And the best way possible was for Kitty to marry a man who didn't love her? Who didn't really want to be married? The idea completely wiped away her appetite and she put down her fork, then dabbed a napkin to her lips.

"I'm sorry, Liam, I'm just not up to eating anything else. Would you mind taking me back to the hotel?"

He eyed her with open concern. "Are you feeling ill?"

"No. It's nothing like that," she quickly dismissed his question. "I'm just tired. It's been a long day and I don't have to tell you that I have a lot to think about."

She could see something like disappointment wash across his face, but he didn't press her to stay and finish the meal. Instead, he said, "Of course. I'll get the waiter to bring the check."

Five minutes later they were back in Liam's truck, traveling down the freeway to the hotel where she would be living during the Hollywood meet.

As he maneuvered through the heavy traffic, they didn't speak, and as the silence between them stretched into awkward tension, Kitty felt even worse than she had at the restaurant.

"I'm sorry, Liam," she said finally. "I've ruined your dinner."

"You didn't ruin anything. I had plenty to eat."

"I wasn't exactly thinking about your stomach."

The grunt he made had her glancing over at him and she was relieved to see a groove of amusement creasing his cheek. At least he wasn't thinking she needed to be taken directly to a psychiatrist's couch for her mood swings.

"Lately I've had brothers and sisters having babies right and left. Pregnancy isn't easy for you ladies or us men."

He should know, Kitty thought. He'd already dealt with

a pregnant wife. Only he didn't have either wife or child now, she thought sadly. And suddenly she was wondering how far along his wife had been in her pregnancy when she'd been killed. As far as Kitty was now?

The question caused her hand to slip to the growing mound of her stomach. She loved this baby so much. So much.

"That stuff you were saying about our baby needing both parents—I know you're right. I'm sure I would be a much better person if I'd had a mother around to balance my life."

He kept his gaze on the traffic. "There's nothing wrong with the person you are now."

She sighed as she smoothed the fabric of her dress over her crossed knees. "I would have been different if my mother had stayed in the family. I seriously doubt I would be a racehorse trainer, spending my every waking hour at the barn or track. I'd probably be working at some office job and have a nice, neat boyfriend who wore chinos and loafers and played golf on the weekends."

"That doesn't sound like you at all."

"I'd be screaming with boredom," she admitted, then darted a glance at him. "When I was fourteen my father offered to let me go to Atlanta to live with my mother. He figured by then I was old enough to decide if I wanted something different in my life."

"Did you go?"

"Only for short visits," she admitted. "By then the bond with my mother was gone, ruined by the distance between us, I suppose. And horses already ran deep in my blood. I knew that when I grew up I wanted to be a successful trainer just like my father."

A grin lifted one corner of his mouth. "And you are. You're just much prettier than he was."

Sad emptiness swept through her and she desperately fought to push it aside. She had to put the past behind her. She had to think ahead. Always ahead to the monumental tasks she was now facing.

"I have yet to prove how successful I am. As a daughter, well, I tried with my mother. But the two of us just never fit together. By the time I was eighteen we'd drifted apart completely."

"What about now?"

"I rarely ever hear from her. She married a man who had two sons. They're grown now and she and her husband travel most of the time. Whenever I do talk to her it's like I'm visiting with a stranger. You know what I mean? Like when a distant relative suddenly calls or shows up and you don't know them from Adam. But just because they're located somewhere on your family tree you feel like there should be a connection and then you feel guilty when there's not one."

"Yeah. I've been there," he said. "And I don't want that to happen with our child. She or he is going to know the both of us. When it thinks of its parents, it's going to think of us as a couple—a united family unit."

If that could only be true in every sense of the word, Kitty thought. But theirs was hardly a normal relationship built on love and devotion. And it never would be. How could they ever hope to be a united family unit?

"You're painting a nice, tidy picture, Liam. But you've not had time to think this all through. Whenever you do you'll realize you can't force something like that."

He shot her a wry look. "Kitty, I have no intention of forcing you to marry me. You'll either agree to become my wife or you won't. It's that simple."

Neat and practical with everything black and white. Every particle in Kitty's heart cringed from the very idea.

But this wasn't about her or her wants anymore, she told herself. There were three people involved in this. The most important being the baby presently growing in her womb.

He turned into the hotel parking lot, but rather than pull up to the front entrance, he found a parking space and cut the engine.

"I'll walk you to your room," he said.

She wanted to tell him that she didn't need an escort. She wanted to remind him of what had happened the last time he'd walked her to her hotel room. But she kept all of that to herself as he skirted around the front of the truck and helped her to the ground.

The night had cooled considerably since they left the training barn. A breeze ruffled the fringe of hair on her forehead and she welcomed it. Being with Liam, having his hand on her arm had heated her whole body. As the doorman opened the glass partition and ushered them inside, she figured her cheeks were flushed a bright pink.

Once they stepped on the elevator, she gave him the floor number. After he punched it and they began to move upward, he stepped closer and studied her face. Beneath the dim glow overhead, his strong features were slightly shadowed and oh, so sexy.

"Are you okay?" he asked.

Her gaze landed squarely on his lips and the urge to kiss him clawed at her, forcing her to swallow before she could speak. "Yes. Why do you ask?"

To her surprise his hand lifted and his fingers gently trailed across her forehead. The soft touch caused her breath to pause and she wondered how he would react if she closed the few inches of space between them and pressed her lips to his.

He said, "You look drained."

She told herself to breathe and relax, but his nearness

was making her crazy. She'd always wanted this man. And once she'd learned just how thrilling it was to be in his arms, she couldn't forget. She wanted more of him. More than he clearly wanted to give.

"A woman doesn't exactly get a marriage proposal every day." Especially from a man of his stature, she could have added. A man who turned female heads as soon as he walked into a room.

A smile flickered ever so briefly on his face. "I didn't stop to think that the thought of having me for a husband was that disturbing. Maybe I should have told you that I don't snore, I pick up my own socks and I don't need to control the TV remote."

Rolling her eyes, she tried to match his teasing mood. Not for anything did she want him to learn that her heart had been invested in him for a long time now. It would only make him feel more obligated, more trapped.

"As if you watch TV," she scoffed. "I suspect the only time you ever sit down is when you watch the replay of a race or a workout."

The dimple at the side of his mouth deepened. "See, that's why you'd never have to worry about having control of the remote."

It wasn't the remote that Kitty was concerned about; it was her heart and what this man might do to it if she gave him the chance.

The elevator came to a stomach-lurching stop and she unconsciously reached for Liam's arm to steady herself. Quickly, he curled an arm around the back of her waist and as they stepped off the elevator she realized that his bracing touch, though unsettling, was a security that she needed.

For weeks now she'd been surrounded by family and friends, yet she'd felt lost and alone. With Liam near, part of that emptiness went away. And though she wouldn't be loved by him, she'd definitely be taken care of. But was that enough for her? Would it ever be enough?

The question plagued her as they walked down the wide corridor until they reached the very end where her suite was located. Once Kitty pulled the entry card from her handbag, she turned to him.

"Thank you for dinner, Liam. I only wish it…had been under different circumstances."

"Under different circumstances we might not have had dinner."

Sadly, he was right. Without her father acting as a magnet between them and without the baby, he probably wouldn't have used up his evening with her.

She bit back a sigh. "Well, I'm very tired. If you don't mind I'll say good-night here at the door."

Bending his head, he placed a platonic kiss on her forehead. "You will think about everything I said?"

Even though his voice was gentle, he sounded more like a man trying to pitch a business deal rather than woo a woman into matrimony. But what did she expect? This wasn't about love or romance or anything to do with happily-ever-after. This was all about responsibility and practicality.

Unable to hold his gaze, she looked away from him and toward a plate-glass window where the lights of the city stretched endlessly before her. "I'll consider everything you said," she murmured. "And I promise I won't keep you dangling about this."

His hand suddenly cupped the side of her face and she was compelled to turn her gaze back to his. Her heart thudded rapidly as she waited for his response.

"Good night, Kitty."

She tried to smile but the effort was worse than weak.

For one split second she'd thought and hoped he was going to pull her into his arms and tell her that he needed her, wanted her. Dear God, she was becoming delusional.

"Good night," she said in a strained voice, then turned and hurried through the door.

Liam had leased a house in another part of town during his stay in California, but he was too keyed up to confine himself to the quiet rooms tonight. Instead, he drove straight back to the track.

Since it was only Tuesday and live racing wasn't scheduled until Thursday afternoon, the track was inactive. Except for a few security lights, the grandstand and the oval circling the infield of lakes and flowers was dark and silent. However, there were plenty of lights and activities going on around the training barns.

The familiar sights were a soothing balm to Liam. This was his life and this was the place he felt most comfortable. It didn't matter which track he was at, or even what state he was in. The "backside," as it was called by those in the industry, was his home; even more of a home than the Diamond D, where his family resided in the Hondo Valley of New Mexico.

The reality of his feelings often filled Liam with guilt. His parents and siblings were special people. They all loved and supported him and encouraged him in all his endeavors. If he had to say something bad about any of them, he wouldn't be able to come up with even one critical remark.

But he wasn't like them. For the past three or four years that fact had become even more apparent as he'd watched his sisters and brothers all marry the loves of their lives and start families of their own. And with each marriage, each arrival of a new baby, he'd begun to feel more and more out of the family circle.

It didn't matter that they all wanted him to forget the past and begin again with someone new. Liam figured a man had one shot at having true love in his life and his had already come and gone. Getting away and traveling with his horses was the outlet that allowed him to forget that Felicia and the baby had been his one chance at happiness.

He and Felicia had practically grown up together and though she'd not been a gorgeous woman, she'd been pretty in a sweet sort of way. Quiet, easygoing and understanding, that had been his wife's nature. And their marriage had been like warm milk, smooth and comforting. She'd been the very heart of his hopes and dreams. But all of that had ended when she and her mother had decided to go on a shopping trip early one foggy morning and she'd missed a curve on the mountain highway. All three had died instantly when the car had plummeted into a deep ravine.

Now fate, in the form of a baby, was forcing him to face a different future and making him wonder if he'd been wrong about things all along. Maybe there was a second chance for him to have a family, he thought. If only he could find the courage to grab it.

At the entrance of the barn, he flashed his identification at the security guard then headed to the section of the building where his horses were stalled. By the time he'd looked over the first three animals and started through the waist-high gate of the next stall, he stopped in his tracks.

"Andy, what are you doing here? Is something wrong with Kate's Kitten?"

The three-year-old filly was named after his grandmother and was one of the very best in the Donovan barn this season. He was aiming her for the Vanity Handicap in

June with a prep race before that. If anything was wrong with KK, as they affectionately called her, he didn't know if he could take it. Not along with everything that Kitty had thrown on his plate today.

The tall, young man with scruffy auburn hair and a sunburned face smiled broadly at Liam. "Not a thing. She's perfect, Liam. I think she likes it better here than any barn we've had her in before. Must be something about the warmer climate." The groom stroked the dark brown filly's neck. "I just came to talk to her a little. You know, tell her how beautiful she is and how much I love her."

Stepping up to the filly, Liam scratched her between the ears, then bent down and ran his hands up and down her front legs. It was a routine inspection that trainers preformed over and over during the day, often times just to reassure themselves that their precious prodigies were sound and ready to perform.

Liam grunted with amusement. "You're supposed to be talking that stuff to a pretty girl."

"KK is a pretty girl."

"I'm talking about the human female," Liam told him.

The groom walked over to the wall of the stall and, folding his arms against his chest, rested his back against the gray cinderblocks. "Hah. You won't find me messing myself up with one of those. Women are bad news, Liam. They're all about themselves. Me. Me. Me. That's all they talk about, or think about or care about."

Satisfied to find there were no lumps or bumps, swelling or fever, Liam rose to his full height and looked over to his groom. Andy had worked for the Donovan barn for seven or eight years now and during that time, he'd watched a gangly teenager grow into an earnest, hard-working young man.

"How old are you, Andy?"

"Twenty-six. I'm old enough to know all about women and smart enough to stay away from them."

"You're awfully young to sound so jaded," Liam muttered.

Andy shot him a defensive look. "Well, you don't have a wife or girlfriend. So you must think like me."

Felicia and the baby had died seven years ago, not long before Andy had come to work for the Donovans and from the young man's comment, no one had ever told him that Liam had once been married. But that shouldn't surprise him. His family and friends, even the longtime Diamond D employees were careful not to bring up the matter of his marriage and subsequent loss. And suddenly, for the first time ever, Liam wondered if keeping everything wrapped and hidden away had been a mistake. Maybe if he and his family had talked about the tragedy more, he could have done a better job of putting it all behind him.

Turning his gaze back to the filly, Liam wondered why Kitty kept pushing her way into his mind, confusing all the visions and plans he'd once had for the future. She wasn't that special, he mentally argued. She was just a woman he'd happened to have sex with and now she was carrying his unborn child. If she ultimately refused to marry him, the world wouldn't come to an end. It would just feel like it, he thought.

Dear God, what was happening to him? He'd sworn to never take another wife. To think of exposing his heart to that much pain again had always been terrifying. But tonight, when Kitty had told him about the baby, something had clicked in him. He'd felt like a stallion needing and wanting to fight for his brood.

"No. I don't think like you, Andy. I don't consider all women bad and self-centered." He did think of them as potential heartaches, though, but that was something Andy didn't need to know. He gave the filly one last pat on the neck then turned to leave the stall. "Did she eat up her supper?"

"Every grain."

"What about her water?"

"Most of it."

"Good." He asked the groom several questions about the other horses in his charge and after Andy had satisfied him that all was okay, Liam started out of the stall. "If you need me, I'll be staying in my office tonight," he tossed over his shoulder.

"You're not going to your place tonight? How come? Me and Clint will see to things here," Andy tried to assure him as he followed Liam out of the stall.

"You don't have to tell me that. I know you will," Liam said. "I just feel like staying here tonight."

Before Andy could say more, Liam strode down the shed row until he reached his office.

Inside, he sat at his desk and pulled out his cell phone. Since he'd gone to dinner with Kitty, eleven voice mail messages had come in along with three text messages. Liam went through them methodically, answering the most urgent ones and leaving reminders to himself to deal with the others tomorrow.

When that was finished, he turned on the computer and went through the schedule that Viveca, the Diamond D racing manager, had put together for him. About a year ago, Liam had finally reached the point where he and his secretary couldn't keep up with all the entries and paperwork involved. Plus, with the number of horses in his stable expanding more and more, he'd needed help in making the best decisions about placing each individual horse in the right race at the right time, which was one of the main missions of a good manager.

He'd not necessarily set out to hire a woman for the job, but Viveca had been in the business for a long time and she knew her stuff. When she'd divorced her husband, an East Coast trainer, she'd been looking for a job and a home. Liam had given her one on the Diamond D and never once regretted it.

But Liam could truthfully say there'd not been much he'd done in his life that he had regretted. Most all the choices he'd made, he'd made for reasons that had been basic and solid. He'd never been an impulsive type of guy. Even his courtship and marriage to Felicia had been long and carefully thought out. They'd started dating in high school and gotten married after both of them had graduated college. Their marriage had been predictable and tranquil with no surprises or conflicts.

So what had happened to him? He'd fallen in bed with a woman he'd never so much as kissed before. His behavior that night had been impulsive and reckless and totally out of character. It didn't matter that he'd been acquainted with Kitty for several years, or that he was somewhat attracted to her. He shouldn't have lost his head. But something about the woman had made him behave in ways he couldn't understand or explain.

Now, incredibly, there was a baby on the way. And yet, he somehow couldn't regret that fact. A few years ago, when his brothers, Brady and Conall, had married and started having children of their own, he had been thrilled for them. But he'd also felt rock-bottom empty. Only God knew how much he'd longed to have a child of his own, to be a father like his brothers. And now, right or wrong, he was going to be.

But would he be a father in every sense of the word? That was the question that was rolling round and round in his mind. He didn't want to fight Kitty about this. And he certainly didn't want to hurt her. Proposing marriage had been another impulsive act on his part, but from his perspective, he'd had no other choice.

His future was now in Kitty's hands and all he could do was wait to see what she intended to do with it. For a man who liked to always be in control, the idea was twisting him in knots and he seriously doubted he'd get a wink of sleep tonight.

He was shutting off the computer and considering taking another walk down the shed row, when a knock suddenly sounded at the door.

Fearful that one of the grooms had discovered a horse in distress, he hurried over to open it. But when the door swung back he found Kitty standing on the threshold, staring solemnly up at him.

She was bundled in a black jacket, her blond hair pulled back in a ponytail, her face totally clean of makeup. She looked incredibly young and vulnerable and her eyes looked suspiciously red, as though she'd been crying.

His heart clenched as he uttered her name. "Kitty! What are you doing here at this late hour? Is anything wrong?"

"I wanted to talk to you. And I didn't know what hotel you were staying in so I took a chance on you being here," she said.

Completely dismayed by her appearance, he said, "You have my telephone number. You could have called me."

She shook her head. "I couldn't say what I have to say over the phone."

Reaching for her arm, he pulled her into the room then shut the door behind them.

"And what is that?"

Her breasts rose and fell as she heaved out a heavy

breath. "That I've made a decision regarding your marriage proposal."

His hand on her arm tightened perceptively. He'd never expected an answer from her tonight. He'd wanted her to weigh the situation and her feelings about it carefully. But apparently she'd made up her mind without too much thought.

He tried to mentally brace himself as he studied her grave expression. "Are you sure, Kitty?"

Her eyes never wavered from his. "Yes. I'm sure that I want to be your wife."

Chapter Four

"Kitty!"

Her name came out in an awed whisper, and as he stared at her, she glanced away from him and swallowed hard. Apparently, she wasn't jumping for joy over the idea of becoming his wife. Strange, he thought, how much that idea hurt. He didn't expect her to suddenly be in love with him. But it would be nice to think she needed and wanted to be with him. Every man wanted that from his wife.

Not waiting for her to say more, he led her over to a small couch that was pushed against the back wall of the room.

"I thought you were going to think about this," he said as he sank down next to her on the burgundy-colored cushions. "I wanted you to think about it before you made a decision."

"So did I," she said in a strained voice. "But after you left the hotel I realized there wasn't much to think about."

"What do you mean?"

Her hand slipped to her stomach and Liam's gaze settled on her fingers as they splayed against the small mound. That was his baby growing there, he thought with amazement. His child nestled snugly in her womb. One day, God willing, he could hold it in his arms, nurture it, love it. Just the idea swelled his chest with emotions. He refused to think about any other possibility, to remember the child he'd once hoped for and lost.

"This baby didn't have a choice about how it came to be. But once it arrives, it seems the least we can do is try to give it a proper home with two parents. It deserves that much from us."

A strange mix of relief and joy was suddenly coursing through him, shocking him with the intensity of his feelings. This wasn't the woman of his dreams, promising to love him forever. It wasn't a time to start handing out cigars and shouting from the rooftop. It wasn't even close. But the happiness inside him refused to run away and hide. He was going to be married and become a father! Tomorrow he might worry that some tragedy would yank it all away from him a second time. But for tonight he was going to allow himself to feel joy.

He must be losing his mind, he thought, as his gaze lifted to the plush pink curves of her lips. He wanted to kiss her, drag her into his arms and hold her tightly against him as if they were a real loving couple.

"You didn't feel that way earlier," he pointed out as he tried to bring himself back to earth. "You said we couldn't force a real family."

"I still believe that," she said, then bending her head, murmured, "but we can try."

"Yes. Try is one thing we both have," he agreed. "We'll have that much going for us—and the baby."

And the baby. Kitty knew that Liam would never let her forget for one minute what this marriage was all about. And maybe that was a good thing, she thought wearily. Maybe she'd never have the chance to let her head drift in the clouds.

Lifting her gaze to his, she said, "Well, that's all I came to say. I'd better get back to the hotel. I have an early morning ahead of me."

He studied her face for long moments and Kitty got the feeling there was much more he wanted to say, but he must have decided it could wait. He quickly rose from the couch and offered her a hand up.

"If you're too tired I'd be happy to drive you back to your hotel," he offered. "The roadways are dangerous and I certainly don't want you to have an accident."

Her wan smile was nothing but grateful. "Thanks, but I'll be careful. The traffic has eased, so I can manage."

He took her hand and pressed it between his two. As his warm fingers wrapped around hers, Kitty had to stifle a sigh. Everything inside of her wanted to lean into him, to rest her cheek upon his chest and let herself believe, if only for a few moments, that he loved her, that he wanted her for a real wife.

"We have a lot to talk about, Kitty. Do you think we could have dinner again tomorrow night? Or maybe we could drive over to the beach tomorrow afternoon?"

Being out in the relaxing sunshine might be the very thing to help give her a positive attitude about the future— their future, she thought. "The beach sounds very nice. I'll try to situate my schedule to have the afternoon free."

"Great," he said with a smile. "I'll do the same."

She made a step to leave and he kept her hand firmly ensconced in his as he strolled with her to the door. Once there, she turned to him.

"Good night, Liam."

One corner of his lips curved upward in a lazy grin. "Is that any way for a newly engaged couple to part for the night?"

Confused, she said, "I don't know what you mean."

His brows arched slightly. "Don't you? I thought a kiss would be more appropriate."

Kiss? Suddenly her heart was hammering. She'd been trying not to let herself think of such things. And she'd certainly never expected his mind to be on such a track. "We, uh, haven't been drinking," she couldn't help but remind him.

"That will make it much nicer, don't you think?"

Bemused by this lighter side of him, she shook her head. "Oh, Liam," she said softly.

The faint smile on his lips was all she could see as suddenly his head bent down to hers and his face grew ever so closer. And then as his lips settled over hers and her eyelids fluttered downward, she could see nothing at all.

But she could definitely feel and the taste of him was exactly as she remembered; his hard mouth just as enticing. Only seconds passed as her senses began to slip and she started kissing him back.

Maybe it was her eager response that caused him to swiftly lift his head or perhaps he'd meant for the meeting of their lips to be nothing more than a brief extension of their goodbye. Either way, Kitty had to wonder what he would think if he knew just how much she wanted him, how many times she'd envisioned him making love to her in the light of day, their minds clear, their hearts beating as one.

"That's a much nicer way to say good-night."

"If you say so," she murmured.

He cast one more long glance at her, then reached to

open the door. Kitty quickly scrambled through the opening before he had a chance to read the longing on her face.

"I'll see you in the morning," she said, then hurried down the dimly lit shed row and away from him.

Before five o'clock the next morning, Liam was sitting at his desk, wolfing down cold pastries and a pot of hot coffee while going over racing schedules and recent workouts. But the time fractions and furlong distances became little more than a jumble of numbers as Kitty continued to push at the fringes of his thoughts.

After a while, he decided to put the work aside and call the Diamond D to give his family the news of his impending marriage.

Fiona, his mother, was the first Donovan to pick up the phone and as soon as Liam blurted out his plans, she very nearly shouted in his ear.

"You're going to do what?"

Leaning back in his chair, he momentarily closed his eyes. "I said I'm getting married, Mom."

"Is there something wrong with this connection? That's the second time I thought you said *married*."

"Nothing wrong with the phone," Liam assured her. "You heard me right."

The silence that followed went on for so long that Liam began to think his mother had fallen over in a dead faint. No doubt he'd shocked her. Nearly seven years had passed since he'd lost Felicia and their baby and that many years since a woman had been in his life. For a long time now his family had pushed and prodded him to find someone to share his life, but he'd stubbornly resisted the idea. Now he could only imagine what a shock this news was going to be to the whole Donovan family.

"Mom? Are you still there?"

"Yes. I—I'm just trying to collect myself, son. You've stunned me."

Liam could have told her that he was pretty stunned himself. In a matter of a day's time he'd learned he was going to be a father and a husband. His head was still reeling from the impact and the changes that were surely about to come to his life.

"In a good way, I hope."

She let out a brief laugh, but Liam could tell it was full of nerves instead of joy. He rubbed his thumb and forefinger against his closed eyelids.

"Well, of course, Liam! I'm happy if you are."

The image of Kitty's face drifted behind his closed eyes. The taste of her lips rose up from his memory. "I am."

There was another pause and then she asked in a perplexed voice, "Do I know this woman you're going to marry? You've not said anything and—"

"You've met her, Mom. It's Kitty Cartwright. Will's daughter."

He heard her soft gasp and realized he'd shocked her all over again. Although, he didn't understand exactly why his mother found this revelation so surprising. It was all very logical to him. Like him, Kitty was a horse trainer. Where else would he have the opportunity to meet a woman besides the track or the training barn?

"Oh. Yes. I remember meeting her at Sunland Park a couple of years ago."

This was not the response he'd expected from his mother. Hell, she, more than anyone in the family, had pestered him about getting married again. But now the tone in her voice implied she was skeptical about Liam's choice of fiancée.

"Is that all you can say?"

"Well, what can I say?" she replied. "I don't really know this girl."

"You might start with congratulations."

"Oh, I'm sorry, Liam," she quickly responded. "Naturally you have my congratulations. It's just that—well, Kitty is very young."

"Yes. But not too young."

"And she's in the same business as you. How is that going to work?"

"Well," he answered brusquely, "she knows how important my job is to me and I understand how essential her position is to her. Since Will died she's stepped up as head trainer for Desert End."

Fiona didn't question his reasoning. Instead, she said, "Yes, Mr. Cartwright's passing was an awful blow to the industry and all who knew him. As I recall, you attended his funeral."

"Yes. I loved Will. And I wanted to be there for Kitty." Even though she'd not appeared to need him at that time, Liam thought grimly. She'd been pregnant with his child even then, but she'd not said a word to him about her condition. The fact still irked him, but he wasn't going to dwell on that now. She'd been in a traumatized state of mind and he could forgive her that much.

"So you two have been seeing each other for a while?" Fiona asked.

For some reason, the image of Kitty naked and writhing beneath him popped into Liam's mind, making it very nearly impossible to focus on his mother's words. "We've been acquainted for six or seven years. But we, uh, didn't start getting close until a few months ago."

"I see. Well, you've certainly done a good job of hiding it. I would've never guessed you had marriage on your mind," she said in a perplexed voice, but then she laughed and her tone changed to a happy one. "So when and where? Tell me all about it. The rest of the family will be plying me for information."

A waiting call was continuing to beep in his ear and the pestering sound reminded him that this hour of morning wasn't the time for a lengthy family conversation. "We haven't decided on the details yet. I'll call you later with all of that, Mom. And I can hear Dad yelling in the background, so you'd better get off and have breakfast."

Fiona agreed and after making her son promise to call back soon, she ended the connection. Liam tossed his phone onto the desk where it immediately began to ring again. But he didn't make a move to answer it. He had to stop his whirling thoughts before he could contend with business calls.

He hadn't had the guts to tell his mother about the baby. But he'd already said enough to get the whole Diamond D buzzing. Besides, there would be time enough before the wedding to tell the family about Kitty's pregnancy.

And then what would they all think? That he was entering some sort of shotgun wedding? That without the coming child, there wouldn't be a wedding at all? That whole notion bothered Liam, although he didn't exactly understand why. He only knew that he didn't want anyone thinking he was being forced into marrying Kitty. Becoming her husband was an honor he was only too glad to accept. That's what he wanted everyone to see.

But if he and Kitty didn't appear to be madly in love, how was anyone going to believe their marriage was anything more than an arrangement of convenience? They'd have to pretend, he concluded. And he had no idea whether she would go along with such a ruse. She'd barely seemed to accept the idea of becoming his wife, much less acting as though she liked it.

With a weary groan, he scrubbed his face with both hands and rose to his feet. He couldn't be worrying about any of it now. Reckless Rendezvous and five other horses were scheduled to work this morning. He needed to give the jockeys their instructions.

Rising to his feet, he shoved his cell phone into his pocket before reaching for a stopwatch and a pair of binoculars. The sun was rising and he had a job to do.

Later that day, at the back of the barn, Kitty was standing beneath a small shade tree with Clayton, a chestnut filly named Pink Sky, and a track farrier. When she'd examined the horse earlier this morning, she'd discovered a small fissure had developed in the toe of her hoof. Kitty hadn't liked the look of it, but the farrier continued to assure her that a new shoe would prevent the crack from spreading.

Kitty could only hope the man was correct. Right now she needed anything positive to hold on to.

"All right, Mr. Johnson. Do what you think is needed," she said. "But right now the turf track is extremely firm. I'm afraid the pounding will spread the crack all the way to the hairline and if that happens I'll have to scratch her off the whole spring meet."

"Don't worry, Kitty. Shep is the best in the business. You can rest assured he'll fix your filly's hoof."

At the sound of Liam's voice all three in the group turned to look at him. And like always, Kitty's heart sped to an excited rush. He was dressed casually in jeans and a pale yellow shirt with the sleeves rolled back on his arms. It wasn't exactly beach wear, but she noticed he had exchanged his usual alligator boots for a pair of smooth brown bull hide.

"Hello, Liam," she greeted.

Instead of giving her a simple hello in return, he walked straight up to her and planted a kiss on her cheek.

Kitty smiled at him and hoped she didn't appear as taken aback as she felt.

"Good morning," he murmured to her then acknowledged the other two men with a nod of his head.

Since Shep Johnson wasn't all that familiar with Kitty, Liam's kiss meant little or nothing to him. But Clayton was staring wide-eyed at the two of them.

If Liam was trying to display some sort of public brand of ownership on her, he'd gotten the job done, she thought drily.

After taking a moment to clear her throat, she promptly set about introducing him to the two men.

"No need for that," Shep said quickly. "I've known Liam for years." He stuck out his hand to Liam. "How are you, old man? Hope you've brought a string of runners this time. California is hurting for more horses."

"Twenty. And I might send for more as the meet goes on," Liam informed the farrier while shaking his big, brawny hand.

"Great," the other man said with a grin, then cast a wink at Kitty. "Better watch him, Ms. Cartwright. He'll beat your—hind end if you're not careful."

She said, "Yes, I'm well aware of Liam's success."

Liam greeted Clayton with a polite handshake then surprised Kitty by curling his arm around the back of her waist. "Kitty isn't worried about me outrunning her," he told the farrier. "Pretty soon, it'll be all in the family. Kitty has agreed to marry me."

Shep Johnson was quick to offer his congratulations to the couple, while Clayton stood there staring at the two of them in disbelief. He'd only learned yesterday that Liam was an acquaintance of the family. Now he was hearing she was marrying the man. No doubt he was wondering what else she was keeping from him. Like the identity of her baby's father.

"You're getting married?" He finally directed the question to Kitty.

Kitty didn't know what Liam was up to or why he'd found it necessary to blurt out their plans so quickly. But no matter the reason, she didn't appreciate his busy mouth. Clayton was her trusted right-hand man. She'd wanted to give him the news in private, where she could assure him that, concerning his position with Desert End, nothing would change.

"Yes, I am," she said, while darting Liam a pointed look. "But we haven't yet set a date."

"I can assure you it will be soon," Liam informed her assistant.

Clayton continued to stare at her, and Kitty could see he was more than stunned, he was offended that she'd kept something so important from him. His gaze slid to her belly and she felt the heat of embarrassment rush to her cheeks.

"Well, it looks like congratulations truly are in order," he said with a strained smile.

Thankfully, someone across the way called to the farrier and the man quickly excused himself from the group. Clayton followed suit, saying he'd better get Pink Sky back to her stall.

"I'll get with Shep in a few minutes and schedule a time to deal with her shoes," he assured Kitty.

"Thanks. And, Clayton, I'll be gone for most of the afternoon, so if you need me for anything just phone or text."

"Right," he said, and then with Pink Sky in tow, he headed into the barn.

Fighting back a weary sigh, Kitty turned to Liam. "Was

all of that necessary?" she asked. "I haven't had time to discuss our engagement with Clayton or any of my staff."

"What difference does it make? They're going to find out soon enough."

"Maybe I should blurt the news to your staff or, even better, your family," she threatened. "And see how you feel."

"I've already told them," he said with a faint grin. "Apparently, I'm more proud of the news than you are."

Proud? Was he? The notion warmed her. At least he wasn't embarrassed to have her become his wife. That had to be a start.

"You've had time for that today? What did you do? Type out a one-sentence announcement and hit the send all button?"

He chuckled. "Hardly. I'm one of those rare people who still prefer to talk instead of push buttons." He gestured toward the barn. "Do you need to collect anything from your office before we leave?"

"Yes. Just give me five minutes and I'll be ready," she assured him.

As she hurried into the barn, she passed Pink Sky's stall and seeing that Clayton was inside the small space, getting the filly settled, she stepped inside.

His expression questioning, the young man looked around at her. "I thought you were leaving," he said.

"I am. I—" Folding her hands behind her back, she stepped deeper into the stall. "I just wanted to say I'm sorry you had to hear about my engagement like that. I'd planned to tell you earlier, but we kept having interruptions and—"

"Forget it, Kitty," he said curtly. "It's none of my business anyway."

"I'm sorry you feel that way, Clayton. Because I don't."

Turning his back to Kitty, he combed fingers through the filly's forelock. "I said you don't have to explain things, Kitty. Who you marry has nothing to do with me."

Hurt laced his voice and as Kitty stared at his back, the notion struck her that he almost sounded jealous. But that couldn't be. He'd never given her any sort of hint that he cared for her in a romantic sense.

"Yes. It is. You're my assistant and you're also my friend. You mean a lot to me," she told him. "And I want you to know that nothing is going to change at Desert End just because Liam and I will be husband and wife."

He glanced over his shoulder at her. "You won't be merging the two barns?"

"Not at all."

"Oh." The tenseness on his face relaxed a bit. "Then I suppose you will need me to stay on," he said.

She patted her belly. "Now more than ever."

With a faint grin, he turned away from the filly and wrapped an arm around Kitty's shoulders. "Okay. If you're happy about this marriage, then I am, too."

Relieved, she smiled at him. The last thing she needed was a strained relationship with her assistant. Without him, she couldn't keep her barn active or her horses running. "Thanks, Clayton. I'm, well, things are changing quickly for me. It's a relief to know that things with you and me will stay the same."

Easing away from him, she started out of the stall. As she was passing through the wire gate, he called out, "You can count on me, Kitty. Always."

She nodded then hurried away to her office. By the time she'd gathered up her bag and sweater and returned to the back of the barn, Liam had walked over to a patch of ground covered with a sparse carpet of green grass. He was conversing with a groom who was leading a horse she recognized from the Diamond D stables.

When she reached him, he arched his brows at her. "I thought you'd decided not to show. Is anything wrong?"

"Sorry," she quickly apologized. "I took a few moments to speak with Clayton."

Reaching for her arm, Liam urged her down a narrow gravel driveway to where his truck was parked. "About your horses? Or about us?"

"Us," she replied. "I don't think he's too happy about your announcement."

"That's not surprising," Liam said flatly. "He obviously has a thing for you."

Kitty shook her head. "Not really. He and I work together. I think he was afraid you might start butting in. I assured him our barns would remain separate."

A grimace crossed his face. "I'm sure by now he's put two and two together and come up with me being the man who got you pregnant—out of wedlock. I can't expect him to look at me in an admirable way. Him or anyone else for that matter," he added.

Surprised, she looked at him. "Why, Liam, I never expected you to be so old-fashioned."

"Old-fashioned?" he practically sputtered.

Sensing he'd taken offense at her comment, Kitty shrugged. "Okay, maybe that's the wrong word. Maybe I should say you're—conventional."

"Well, hell, yes, I'm conventional! I was raised to be a responsible man. I'm not a playboy. Not even close. But I suppose when people look at you they're going to think things like that."

"I seriously doubt anyone will be thinking you're a playboy," she said pointedly. "Or anything close to it. Besides, there are more important things to consider than appearances."

He didn't say anything to that until he'd helped her into the truck and settled himself behind the steering wheel.

"I'm glad you brought up the subject of appearances." He looked at her as he stabbed the key into the ignition. "It's something I want to discuss with you."

She turned slightly toward him. "Why? What does that have to do with anything?"

Instead of starting the engine, he leaned back in his seat and looked at her. "When I spoke to my mother this morning, I realized that—well, for a long time my family has been urging me to marry again. All of them, my parents and siblings are all happy and in love. They want the same thing for me. And now my mother is no doubt spreading the word that I've found it." Sighing, he looked away from him and shook his head. "I guess what I'm trying to say is that I don't want to disappoint them. I'd like for them to think that you and I are a typical couple."

But they weren't typical, she thought sadly. He knew it and so did she. "Ah. I understand. When we're around your family you want us to pretend to be in love and crazy about each other."

"Actually I was hoping we wouldn't limit the pretense to my family. If everyone got the idea that we're in love, they'd come to the conclusion that we didn't have to get married."

So that was the reason for that little kiss on the cheek he'd given her a few minutes ago. She should have known it wasn't a real display of affection for his new fiancée. Her brows arched with disdain. "But we don't *have* to get married. That was your idea."

His jaw tightened. "You agreed to it," he reminded. "Or are you already backing out on your promise?"

Her gaze dropped away from his face to focus on her growing belly. "No. I'm not backing out. Whatever you might think of me, I'm not a quitter. Or an actress," she added then inwardly groaned. Who was she trying to kid? Herself? She didn't have to act like she loved Liam. The feelings were already there. And that was the whole problem, she decided. Her "acting" might be so real he'd get to believing it. And then where would she be? "But I suppose I can try. If it means that much to you."

She glanced over to see visible relief on his face.

"It does. And in the long run I think it will be good for our child."

Good? How could a marriage based on pretense be good for anyone? Especially their child? She wanted to fling the questions at him, but she tamped them down. She had to get a grip on herself. She had to remember that she couldn't let emotions dictate her behavior or even her plans for the future.

A future without love.

Trying to shove that dismal thought away, she said, "I hope you're right, Liam. And I hope that our child never learns that his parents were a pair of phonies!"

He started the engine and gunned the truck onto the driveway. "Sometimes the truth hurts much worse than a lie," he muttered.

Kitty looked out the passenger window and blinked away her tears.

Chapter Five

By the time the Pacific Ocean glimmered in the distance, Kitty had collected herself and was determined to enjoy the sand and surf. Before venturing onto the beach, they purchased hot dogs and drinks from a sidewalk vendor and shared the meal on a nearby park bench.

Although the day was nice and sunny, the sea breeze was brisk enough to have Kitty dragging a soft blue sweater over her white shirt. As they walked along a stretch of empty sand, Kitty focused her gaze on the waves rolling onto the shoreline and the swooping gulls, but her mind was honed in on the man walking beside her. The man who was soon to be her husband.

"So have you thought about the sort of wedding you want?" he asked after they'd traveled only a short distance.

Surprised, she glanced at him. The wind was tousling his brown hair and the sun on his face made his features appear even more tanned. He was one sexy man and just thinking about becoming his wife left her warm all over. "Wedding?" she repeated blankly. "I figured you'd probably want a simple civil ceremony here in Los Angeles County."

His gaze dropped to the sand and their slow-moving footsteps. "I suppose that would legally get the job done. But I'd like for my family to be present and a priest or minister to marry us. Other than that I'll leave it all up to you."

He'd just made an issue of them presenting the image of a loving couple to his family. She should have known he'd want to make their wedding appear to be a sanctified union.

"That's fine with me," she murmured.

Kitty had never been one of those young women obsessed with having an elaborate wedding and all the trappings that went with it, but she had often dreamed of that special day and how it might be. Mostly when she'd imagined her wedding day, she'd thought of her father giving her away and the pride and emotion she would see on his face. He'd always wanted to see her married to a good man. And no matter the situation between her and Liam, there was no doubt in her heart that he was a good man.

All at once she felt so very far from home. From the big Texas sky, the sage and cactus, the smell of the desert after a rain and the horses dozing beneath the shade of a mesquite. Her father had made that beautiful home for her. The least she could do for him now was to be married there.

"I'd like to have the ceremony at Desert End," she said suddenly. "I believe Dad would have wanted that."

Without warning Liam paused and curled an arm around her shoulders. Kitty turned to look at him and as she did, he pulled her to him and rubbed his lips against her forehead. Her breath caught as sweet sensations rippled through her.

"I think you're right," he murmured, his fingers tangling in her windswept hair."

Trying not to tremble or let him see just how much his touch affected her, she said, "Liam, there's no one out here who knows us. You don't have to pretend with me now."

"Who says I'm pretending?"

Her breathing nearly stopped as she carefully scanned his face. "What does that mean?"

His gaze settled on her parted lips. "You're a beautiful woman, Kitty. And we have made a baby together."

Her heart jerked then sped into a gallop. "The wine—you weren't thinking." The breathless sound of her voice betrayed the upheaval he was causing inside of her. "Today you—"

"I had soda with my hot dog," he interrupted with a wry grin. "So I'm thinking now. And kissing my new fiancée doesn't require acting. With a woman like you it's a natural instinct."

His lips moved from her forehead to her cheek and her fingers clutched at the front of his shirt. "Liam, you aren't thinking now."

"And you're thinking too much, Kitty."

Was she? She didn't have time to contemplate the answer as his lips settled over hers and swiftly put a stop to her ability to think at all.

The gulls screeched, the wind sang in her ears and down the beach the happy shrieks of a child mingled with the bark of a dog. But none of those sounds distracted Kitty's senses from Liam's kiss.

It was shameful how much she wanted him, how much her body craved his and how little she could do to hide it. In fact, hiding her desire was impossible as she opened her lips beneath his and slipped her arms around his waist.

As far as Kitty was concerned she could have continued

kissing him for long, long minutes. Wrapped in his arms, his mouth against hers, it was easy to let herself believe he was kissing her with love.

But the embrace came to an abrupt halt as something suddenly smacked against Kitty's leg and voices sounded only steps away.

The intrusion instinctively parted their heads and Kitty glanced around to see a young woman chasing after a small girl around the age of five. At the moment, the child had one thing on her mind and that was to retrieve the yellow beach ball that had rolled to a stop near Kitty's and Liam's feet.

"I'm so sorry," the woman called out to them. "My daughter's aim isn't very good. Especially in this wind."

"No problem," Liam assured the woman. Reaching down, he retrieved the ball and tossed it to the dark-haired girl.

Somehow the child managed to grab the ball in midair and once she'd secured her hold, she took off in a joyous run. A chocolate lab raced behind her, barking enthusiastically at the game of tag.

Suddenly, the girl paused long enough to shout back at them. "Thank you!"

"Yes, thanks," the mother added before hurrying to catch up with her daughter.

Kitty wistfully watched the trio head on down the beach while Liam curved his hand against the back of her waist.

"She's an adorable little thing," he remarked, then glanced thoughtfully down at Kitty. "Would you prefer a daughter?"

"Boy or girl doesn't matter," she said, her gaze still on the family. "I was just wondering about her father."

"We don't even know if she has one," he said. "At least one that shares the same home."

She glanced up at him. "That's what I mean. Is he around to love and care for her—like mine was for me?"

"Let's hope so." His hand slid around her side until he was touching her stomach. "One thing you can be sure of, I'll be around for our son or daughter."

Her gaze flickered back to his face and like a magnet it was instantly drawn to his lips. For a brief moment his kiss had felt so deep and full of need. Or had that been her own passion blurring her senses from the truth? Oh, God, she couldn't keep weighing and analyzing his every word and every touch, she told herself. She'd have a mental breakdown before she ever said the words *I do*.

Trying to swallow the thickness in her throat, she asked, "So when do you want to have this wedding? I'll need a bit of time to get things organized at the ranch. Natalie will handle most of it for me. So I'll probably fly there a day or two beforehand."

"Who's Natalie? A relative?"

Kitty shook her head. "Other than my aunt Renee I don't have any female relatives near El Paso. Natalie is my racing manager. But most of the time she ends up managing any and every sort of problem or event that comes up on the ranch. I'm sure this one is going to be a big surprise to her."

His lips took on a wry twist as he urged her into a leisurely stroll toward a small sand dune. "Surprise is a mild description of my mother's reaction to the news this morning. I very nearly sent her into shock."

"What about the rest of your family? I know you have five siblings. Did you talk with any of them?"

"I didn't have time. Besides, I knew as soon as I ended the call Mom would be on a mega speaker, spreading the word. And what about your brother?" he asked. "Have you told him yet?"

At the mention of her brother, Owen, Kitty inwardly stiffened. Although she loved her brother, their relationship was not an easy one. Especially since their father had died and the will had been read.

Oh, God, the will. Since she'd seen Liam yesterday, she'd been trying not to think about the impossible burden her father had heaped upon her. And she'd not had time to contemplate just how Liam might react to her problems or even if she should tell him about the issue. Right now the baby was her first concern and it was Liam's only concern. The ranch couldn't enter into the tenuous relationship she had with this man.

Trying to sound casual, she said, "He's been working the night shift here lately. I don't like to wake him, unless it's an emergency. I'll give him the news later."

And she was definitely dreading Owen's reaction. He'd already made it clear that he wasn't pleased about her condition. Not that he had anything against single mothers or that he blamed her for being reckless. No, he'd already decided that the father was a first-class jerk for not stepping up to the plate. What was he going to think when he learned it was Liam Donovan?

Owen had never met Liam face-to-face, but he'd heard enough about him from their father. Will had painted Liam as a damned smart trainer and a man to be respected. But Owen had his own opinions about people and she could only hope he would see the goodness in Liam and welcome him into their small family. But she had her doubts about that. Liam was in the horse-racing business and that in itself was enough to make Owen dislike him.

"Well, I'm not sure how your racing schedule is this April, but mine won't get into full swing until the third week of this month. I could manage to be away from the barn any time before that," he said.

"I'll contact Natalie this evening and go over my schedule. Maybe I can have everything ready in two weeks. Are you agreeable to that?"

He grimaced. "You sound like you're planning a business meeting instead of a wedding."

Vaguely surprised by his comment, she cast him a pointed look. "In our case it is business. Baby business."

Reaching up, he touched a finger to her cheek. The simple touch warmed her face far more than the sun and she could feel a blush tinge her face with color.

"In a manner of speaking," he replied. "So what are we going to do about a honeymoon?"

Honeymoons were for lovers, she wanted to say. And she couldn't imagine bearing the pain of spending several days in some romantic place while her husband pretended to be madly in love with her.

She released a short laugh to mask her sadness. "I don't think our wedding warrants a honeymoon. And neither of us can really afford to be away from the horses for any length of time."

He let out a heavy breath and Kitty wondered if the reaction was one of relief or disappointment.

Don't be a ninny, Kitty, the man is relieved. He's hardly the sort of guy who'd choose to entertain a woman for several days when he can be with his horses instead. Especially when he doesn't love the woman.

"You're right. It would take some maneuvering with our schedules. But, well, every bride deserves a honeymoon. I don't want to cheat you out of the experience."

Bride. It felt strange to hear him use that particular word. She didn't think of herself as soon becoming a bride. Her name would change to Donovan and there would be a piece of paper declaring them man and wife. Other than that, what could possibly change?

Wiping her windswept hair away from her face, she looked out at the rolling waves. "I don't expect you to treat me like a new bride, Liam. Besides, a honeymoon requires traveling and I get plenty of that with our job. And let's face it…I'm not exactly in the perfect condition right now for such a trip."

"Well, if that's the way you feel about it," he said. "We can always act coy and tell our families we're planning to take a honeymoon after the baby is born—when you feel more up to it."

Unable to bite back the sarcasm on her tongue, she glanced at him. "Might as well. Everything else about the marriage will be phony. Let's have a pretend honeymoon to go along with it."

"Kitty."

There was censure in the way he spoke her name, but Kitty also picked up a hint of disappointment threaded through his voice. And the idea left her feeling a little ashamed of herself. Marriage, even if it wasn't borne of love, wasn't something to be mocked.

She sighed. "I'm sorry, Liam. I shouldn't have said any of that. I've not exactly been myself these past few days. And all of this planning—it's more than I can take in."

His hand gently rubbed the side of her arm. "I'm the one who should be apologizing, Kitty. I expect you to just fall in with all of this as though it's an everyday thing." His hazel-green eyes softened as he studied her face. "I'm sorry. Because I should understand this is not the way you'd planned or imagined things would be for you. But I believe that later on you'll be glad of all these decisions we're making now."

If a woman was lucky she got married once in her life

to the man she loved with all her heart. This had to be her one time. But years from now, when their baby was grown, would they still be man and wife? She didn't want to think about the answer.

"I truly hope so, Liam."

Near the end of April, on a Tuesday afternoon, Kitty understood why it had been so important to let Liam's family believe they were in love and marrying for all the right reasons. She'd never seen such a happier group of people. The Donovans had all traveled to West Texas to see Liam get married. His parents, Doyle and Fiona, Grandmother Kate, his two brothers, Conall and Brady, and three sisters, Maura, Dallas and Bridget, plus a host of children ranging in ages from four years to infancy.

The big house at Desert End had seen parties before with laughing guests clearly enjoying themselves. But this was all very different for Kitty. This was a huge family, something that she and Owen knew nothing about. And the idea that she was just minutes away from becoming a part of Liam's vast family was almost overwhelming. And as she stood in her bedroom in front of a full-length mirror, nagging qualms were trying to shred holes in her decision to marry him. Above everything, she didn't want to hurt or disappoint Liam or his family. She wanted to be a part of them in a real sense. Just as much as she wanted to be Liam's *real* wife and the first and most important thing in his heart.

"You don't think the neckline of my gown is too revealing, do you?" Kitty asked as she thoughtfully stared at her image. The dress she'd chosen was champagne-colored silk with an overlay of white, rose patterned lace. The V-neck plunged to the valley between her breasts, while the long, close-fitting sleeves came to a point on the

tops of her hands. An empire waist with subtle gathering
gently camouflaged her expanding waistline and though
everyone was telling her she looked gorgeous, she could
only wonder what Liam was really going to think about
her appearance. Two weeks ago on the beach he'd called
her beautiful and she'd held on to those words like a ray
of hope. Now doubts and nerves were setting in, making her wonder if she was about to leap into a lion's den.

"Not at all," Fiona scoffed away her question. "You look
very feminine and beautiful. Liam is going to be mesmerized by the sight of you."

As Fiona fastened a string of pearls at the back of Kitty's neck, she felt the woman's joy spreading into her and
it helped to calm the nervous flutter in her stomach.

"I think she's already mesmerized Liam," Kate spoke
up from across the bedroom. "I haven't seen my grandson
looking this happy in a long, long time."

"Neither have I." Fiona let out a little laugh as she gave
Kitty's shoulders a brief hug. "We'd all thought Liam had
given up on love and marriage. And all this time he had
you! But he's always been one to keep things to himself.
Even as a little boy."

Kitty returned the two women's smiles. How could she
not? They'd been so warm and welcoming, so delighted
over the fact that a baby was on the way. They could have
accused her of trapping Liam, of being a gold digger or
worse. Right after she'd agreed to become Liam's wife,
the idea that the Donovans might be concerned about her
motives had entered Kitty's mind. She'd suggested to Liam
that he might want to have a prenup drawn up to protect
his interest in the Diamond D, but he'd dismissed the idea,
saying he trusted her to always be fair with him. Apparently the rest of his family trusted her, too. Kate, Fiona

and all the Donovans had been more than welcoming and had openly thanked her for making Liam happy.

But oh, God, was he happy? Since he was bound to put on a good front for his family, Kitty couldn't guess what he was actually feeling today. But sooner or later, his real feelings were bound to show and thinking of that time scared her.

Yet today she was going to do her best not to think about the future. This was her wedding day and as far as she was concerned, Liam was the only husband she would ever have in her lifetime.

"Well, I didn't have time to have a dress sewn," she said with a nervous laugh. "Actually, I haven't had time to do much at all. Liam's been rushing me."

Rising from a cushioned armchair, Liam's grandmother smoothed down her pencil skirt. For a woman in her eighties, Kate looked and acted decades younger. Kitty was amazed by her, especially when she'd learned that Kate made it a daily routine to go horseback riding every morning.

"Just like a man," Kate said with a chuckle. "I hope he doesn't plan on rushing your honeymoon."

Glancing away from the older woman, Kitty toyed with the braided chignon at the back of her head. "No. There won't be any rush concerning our trip," Kitty said, hoping she didn't sound too evasive. "Liam and I decided it would be best if we put our honeymoon off until the baby is born and our racing schedules quiet down."

"Oh. Well, that makes sense. I—"

The rest of Kate's sentence was halted by a sharp knock on the door and she quickly strode across the room to answer it. After a brief moment she returned to where Fiona was pinning a white Camilla to Kitty's hair.

"It's your brother, Kitty. He says everything is ready whenever you are."

Nodding nervously, Kitty tried to smile, but found herself dangerously close to tears. "Well, I guess this is it."

"You look lovely, Kitty," Fiona assured her.

"You also look a bit shaky. Here, take my arm," Kate ordered as she thrust a sturdy elbow at Kitty.

Flanked by the two women, Kitty left the bedroom to find Owen standing out in the hallway waiting to escort her to the back of the house where the ceremony would be taking place in the courtyard.

After Kate handed her over to Owen, she and Fiona quickly excused themselves. Once Kitty was alone with her brother, she clung tightly to his arm.

"Kitty," he said with an awed hush. "You look more beautiful than I've ever seen you."

Owen was a tall, sinewy dark-haired man with features that resembled his late mother's. As a lawman, he naturally exuded strength and authority and this was one time Kitty was glad to lean on him.

"Thank you, brother."

"If Dad was here he'd be beaming," he told her.

Kitty cast him a skeptical look. Pleasing her father and making him proud had always been important to her, even when they'd fought over certain aspects of her life. She could only hope and pray he was smiling down at her now. "You think so?"

"Where you were concerned, he always beamed."

In spite of their many clashes, she and Owen had always managed to speak their minds with each other and she didn't hesitate now. "It's obvious you're not overjoyed about this marriage."

He grimaced as he glanced out the window. Since the minister wasn't yet in place, he decided he had time to reply. "Sorry but that's the way I feel, Kitty. Hell, this has all been so quick. You've been pregnant for nearly seven months and you've not seen fit to tell me that Liam Donovan was the father. That tells me you were uncertain about him or maybe yourself. Then you go out to California for a few days and suddenly you're telling me you're getting married."

"I realize it seems sudden. But—"

"Sudden! Kitty, you're not an impulsive person. And the way I see it, you'd already waited this long. You could have waited and thought about it a bit more."

She practically glared at him. "I wanted you to give me away today because Dad is gone. You're my brother and the only close relative I have left. I'd hoped for this one special day in my life you'd try to show me a bit of love. I guess I forgot that you're hell-bent on hurting me."

"I've always loved you. That's why I'm trying to warn you."

"Yeah. That's what Dad always said, too."

His lips clamped together. "This isn't a time for us to be fighting. We've already talked about this last night. There's no point in hashing it over again."

"I'd just like to know why you have to oppose everything I do?" she asked in a low, gritty voice. "Why can't you be happy for me?"

He shot her a dark look. "I would be happy for you if I thought it was the real thing. But this marriage is all about this ranch, the horses and your desperation to hang on to everything. I know this and you know it. And so will Liam, eventually. But don't worry, sis. I won't bring it up today or any other day. You're going to hang yourself without me having to open my mouth."

Kitty momentarily closed her eyes. "Oh, Owen, please stop."

He reached over and covered her hand with his and her eyes opened to see that his expression had suddenly softened.

"Look, sis, you don't need Liam Donovan. You don't need Black Dahlia or any of those damned horses."

"I know what I need, Owen. And no one is twisting my arm to do anything. I love Liam. Really love him." She stared unwaveringly at her brother. "That might not mean anything to you. But I hope to God that someday it will."

He studied her for a moment longer and then with a sigh of resignation, he bent and placed a kiss on her forehead. "All right, sis. All right. But just remember—if Liam Donovan doesn't treat you right, I'll break his damned neck."

With that threat ringing in her ears, Owen led her through a pair of wide French doors and out to a large courtyard where Liam and the minister were waiting against a backdrop of blue, blue sky, endless flowers and a tinkling bronze fountain sculpted in the shape of racing horses.

As Kitty and her brother walked through a narrow aisle of seated guests, Kitty was vaguely aware of the wedding march being played on a violin, the soft breeze blowing against her cheeks, the sturdy support of Owen's arm, and the glances from family and friends as she moved forward. But none of those things could distract her focus away from Liam.

A Western-cut suit hugged his tall form and silhouetted the lean, muscular shape of his body, while the chocolate color of the fabric set off the rich subtle streaks of gold and chestnut in his brown hair. But it was the expression on his face as he watched her move toward him that had her heart beating fast, her gaze locking with his. Something in his eyes, some fleeting emotion grabbed her and then she felt the baby move. The baby that they had made together.

By the time she reached Liam's side and Owen handed her over to him she was trembling. And when he enveloped her right hand in his, tears stung the back of her eyes. He might not love her, she thought, but he did care. And for now, for this special moment in her life, that was enough.

Chapter Six

Five hours later, their plane landed at LAX. A short time after that they were ensconced in Liam's truck, driving away from the busy airport. Their flight from El Paso had been short and uneventful. For the most part, Kitty had been quiet during the trip and Liam couldn't decide if she was merely tired from all the traveling and hustle and bustle, or if she was thinking about the wedding and wishing she'd not gone through with it.

Now as he maneuvered the vehicle through the heavy freeway traffic, he flexed his tense shoulders and glanced over at her. She was relaxed in the seat, the back of her head resting against the soft leather.

Dressed in a long skirt and thin sweater that matched, she looked very pretty. But the image of Kitty in her wedding gown with flowers in her hair was one that he knew he'd never forget. As she'd stood beside him and repeated the vows the minister had read, her beauty had practically taken his breath. He'd felt humbled that she was becoming his wife, grateful that she was having his child, and frightened by the intensity of his emotions.

Even now, just thinking about their kiss as man and wife clogged his throat and left him feeling like a sentimental fool. Like she'd said, they'd never been a couple before and she wasn't marrying him for love, yet he was letting himself think of their marriage in those terms.

"Are you feeling okay?" he felt compelled to ask.

She gave him a wan smile. "Yes. Just a little tired."

"We'll be home in just a few minutes," he assured her.

And then what? he wondered. She was his wife and though they'd chosen not to go to some exotic isle for a honeymoon, they were still newlyweds. How was she expecting things to be with them? Platonic? With the two of them merely sharing space like two roommates just tolerating each other's presence?

Hell, Liam, what are you expecting from the woman? She's only been in your bed once and since then all you've done is kiss her a few times. You think that's enough to make her want to fall into your arms?

No, he should give her time, Liam mentally argued with himself. Time to get used to the two of them living as man and wife. Time to get accustomed to the idea of sharing the same name and same bed.

But oh, Lord, keeping his hands off her was going to be tough. Ever since he'd kissed her that day on the beach, he'd wanted her. And the days since then hadn't dimmed his desire. In fact, the passing time had deepened his craving.

"I hope your girls got the kitchen stocked," she said. "The wedding cake was delicious, but I couldn't eat much."

His girls meant Olivia and Edyta, the two hot walkers he'd brought with him to Hollywood. He sometimes asked them to do personal chores, if they could find time to break away from their barn duties, which mainly consisted of walking the horses by hand. Before he and Kitty had left for El Paso he'd given the two young women a list filled with groceries and household items, a credit card to purchase everything and the key to his house in the Westchester community. Liam was hoping Liv and Edie, as he called his two girls, had managed to get everything in place and in order for their arrival.

"You didn't have much chance to eat," he said, "Everyone was coming at you from all directions with kisses and congratulations."

He glanced her way just in time to see the corners of her mouth tilt downward.

"I'm sorry we didn't have much of a reception," she said quietly. "Your family must have been disappointed. They'd traveled all that way and I'm sure they would have enjoyed some music and dancing and delicious food. Instead, they got a slice of cake and a swig of punch and a quick goodbye from us before we had to make the plane."

"Don't worry about it. There will be other occasions where we can celebrate. Something festive is always going on at the Diamond D. Especially at Christmas. And the baby will be here then."

She sighed. "I've never experienced a Christmas without Dad. It's not going to be easy. But I'm hoping the baby will fill most of the void."

The more time he was with Kitty, the more he realized how much her life had revolved around her father's. And he was beginning to wonder if the man had kept a restraining hand on his daughter, or at least tried to. He'd loved Will and the man had known the racing industry inside and out. But that didn't mean he'd been perfect.

Wanting to reassure her, he reached over and squeezed her hand. "We have a lot to look forward to, Kitty."

"I hope you're right," she said.

From the corner of his eye, Liam saw her head bow and her fingers absently fiddled with the heavy gold band he'd placed on her finger during the wedding. The pensive sight troubled him, but he hardly knew what to do about it. He could only hope that with a little time she would accept the idea of being his wife.

"I've not talked that much with you about your brother," he said as they neared the street where their house was located. "He seems to care about you very much."

"Sometimes too much."

"What does that mean?"

"He's a whole lot like Dad. He thinks he knows what's best for me and he gets annoyed when I don't go along with his thinking."

"Hmm. And what does he think about you marrying me?" Liam asked.

He could feel her gaze sweeping over the side of his face as he steered the truck into the driveway.

"Why are you asking me that?" she questioned. "You talked with him. Surely you could tell whether he liked you."

Grunting with wry humor, Liam killed the engine. "*Like* would be stretching it, Kitty. But I'm not going to let Owen bother me."

She sighed. "You shouldn't take my brother personally. It's nothing against you, Liam. He thinks I'm incapable of making sound decisions, that's all."

He turned slightly to look at her. "And he thinks he could make better ones for you? Like not marrying me?"

A tight grimace twisted her lips. "He says he'll break your neck if you treat me badly."

Liam chuckled. "He must be more like Will than I thought. I think I'm going to like him."

She looked at him with surprise. "It doesn't make you angry that he made such a threat?"

"No. I'd say the same about my brothers-in-law. Even though I like all three of them, I'd enjoy breaking a jaw if he hurt my sister."

With that he exited the truck then walked around to the passenger door to help her down. Once she was on the ground and standing close to him, he considered pulling her into his arms and kissing her. But already her gaze was straying to the front of the house and Liam quickly decided that whenever he did kiss her, he wanted her undivided attention. He wanted her focus to be on him and nothing else.

Tucking an arm around the back of her waist, he guided her forward across a small lawn landscaped with palm trees and flower beds. Massive bougainvilleas grew to the rooftop of the ranch style house and shrouded a portion of the ground level concrete porch. Except for the distant bark of a dog, the neighborhood was dark and quiet.

It wasn't a tropical island, Liam thought as he unlocked the door, but here they would be alone for the very first time. What was she expecting from him? Wanting from him? At the wedding and in front of their families, they'd been pretending to be in love. But once they'd gotten on the plane and headed to California, she'd withdrawn from him. Was she trying to tell him that she wanted him to keep his distance? Or was she simply wondering what was next for them?

"It's good to be home," she murmured as he pushed open the carved oak door.

Liam hadn't been expecting her to call the house their

home and something about the word and the way she said it gave him the courage to turn and reach for her.

She gasped softly as he lifted her in his arms and cradled her against his chest. "I totally agree," he said softly. "Welcome home, Mrs. Donovan."

"Liam! What are you doing?"

Smiling down at her, he stepped into the house and kicked the door shut behind them.

"Carrying my new bride across the threshold," he told her.

From a nearby window there was just enough light from a streetlamp filtering through the blinds to allow him a glimpse of her face. A shadow lay across one eye and part of her lips, but it didn't hide the surprise he saw there. Or stem the longing he had to bend his head and kiss her.

"Oh, Liam," she whispered. "I'm not a real bride."

He lowered his face to hers. "You feel very real to me."

As he settled his lips over hers, she made a needy groan low in her throat. At the same time he felt her arms slipping around his neck and the enticing invitation thrilled him, spoke to him as no words could have and before he could temper his desire, his lips were hungrily plundering hers, his arms crushing her even closer to his chest.

He wanted to absorb the taste of her into his senses, pull the intense pleasure inside him so that he could carry it with him forever. But after a while the pressure of her weight on his arms became too great and his lungs burned for a breath of fresh oxygen.

Forcing himself to break the kiss, he quickly carried her though the house until they reached the master bedroom. Inside the large space, a night-light was burning in one corner, illuminating a path to the king-size bed. Once Liam reached it, he set Kitty on her feet, but kept his hands firmly anchored on her shoulders.

"I'm not sure how you feel," he whispered. "But it feels like our wedding night to me."

Reaching up, she cradled his face between her palms and for a moment he saw raw emotion flicker in her eyes.

"Yes," she softly agreed. "Our wedding night."

Bending his head, he brushed his lips against her forehead. She smelled sweet, like a May flower and beneath the fabric of her sweater, the warmth of her flesh seeped into his hands. Just to be touching her in this simple fashion left him trembling with desire and aching for more of her. He was tumbling head over heels down a steep cliff, he thought, without any sign of a handhold to catch himself.

"I want to make love to you, Kitty. To lie beside you and sleep with you. Until I carried you through that door a few minutes ago, I didn't realize just how much I wanted those things," he admitted.

"I want the same things, too, Liam. And we are man and wife now," she added, as though she needed to justify having sex with her husband.

He pushed his fingers into the fine hair at her temple and stroked the golden strands away from her forehead. "We're going to make this work, Kitty," he murmured. "We're going to be happy. Together."

Before the last of her sigh slipped past her lips, Liam bent his head to kiss her again. She clung to him and he wondered if her reaction was from desire or desperation. But in the end, he decided it didn't matter. He wanted his wife. In every way.

"Kitty," he whispered, when their lips finally parted. "Are you okay? I mean—will this be safe for you and the baby?"

"Don't worry." She began to undo the buttons on his shirt. "The doctor assured me it would be fine."

With a groan of relief, he laid her gently onto the mattress then joined her, clothes and all.

After his mouth once again found hers, his hands delved beneath the hem of her sweater and slipped upward until he was touching the warm flesh above the waistband of her skirt. Her soft skin fed his senses and as his hands moved toward her breasts, he could hardly contain the desire that was threatening to overtake him.

This wasn't like him. He never lost control. Never wanted anything this much. The desperate thoughts tore through his mind as the need to undress her and have her naked in his arms forced him to tear his mouth from hers.

As he pulled the cashmere fabric over her head, she said in a low voice, "Please don't expect me to look like I did when— Well, a few months ago."

Tossing the sweater aside, he drew back far enough to look at her and as his gaze met her blue one, his chest swelled with emotions that threatened to choke him. "Kitty, you're beautiful," he whispered hoarsely, his hands gently roaming her thickening belly. "The way you look makes me happy. Very happy."

"Liam."

His name was the only word she uttered as he pulled away her skirt, then bent his head to press kisses to the precious mound of their baby. Up until now he'd not attempted to get this close to her. But he'd very much wanted to. And now that his cheek was pressed against her, his lips caressing her skin, the baby felt very real to him. No longer was it just an image of the future or a precious hope in his heart. It was a tiny person living and breathing within the safety of this woman's womb. And he loved it. Oh, how he loved it.

The moment Liam had swept Kitty up in his arms, she'd lost control of her emotions and the barrier she'd tried to erect around her heart had tumbled down like a sandcastle at high tide. Something about his touch affected her in ways she didn't understand and all she could do was react and relish the pleasure of being close to him.

Now as he pressed warm kisses over her bulging belly, tears stung her eyes and thickened her throat. He might not ever love her, she realized, but she was certain he loved the baby and that fact alone was enough to melt her heart.

Thrusting her hands into his hair, she urged his mouth up to hers and she kissed him hungrily while the heavy weight of her wedding ring reminded her that she belonged to this man. In more ways than she wanted to think about.

When their lips finally parted and he began to nuzzle a trail down the side of her neck, she whispered, "I need to be honest, Liam. That night we went to bed together it wasn't the wine. Not on my part."

The honesty in her voice must have snagged his attention because he lifted his head to stare at her. "What are you trying to tell me?"

A faint smile curved her lips as she fumbled with the last two buttons on his shirt. "That I wasn't tipsy. I knew exactly what I was doing."

The fronts of his shirt fell away and he gasped sharply as she flattened her hands against his abdomen.

"That's hard to believe," he said in a strained voice.

She moved her hands up and down his rib cage, loving the feel of each bump and curve of his corded muscles. "You're a very sexy man, Liam Donovan," she said thickly. "I've thought so for a long, long time."

One of his brows arched with surprise and then a crooked grin slowly spread his lips. "Why didn't you let me in on your secret?"

Because he was the sort of man she'd been trying to

avoid, she thought. He was the dangerous kind; the sort that kept his heart locked away.

She sighed. "I didn't think it would make any difference. You've never exactly looked at me like you wanted me."

He lowered his head and brushed his lips against her cheek. "I've always thought you were a beautiful young woman, Kitty. But that night after dinner—when I walked you to your room and we ended up in bed—that's when it dawned on me how much I wanted you. And my desire had nothing to do with the wine. I could have repeated the alphabet backward, counted to a hundred in Spanish and walked a chalk line."

She halted her roaming hands as she pondered his admission. "I suppose we both wanted to hide our behavior behind the wine."

"Well, we don't need to hide how we feel anymore, do we?"

He was talking about sex, of course. And that much she couldn't hide from this man. Not when the simple touch of his hand melted every cell in her body.

"I'm not going to try," she murmured.

He gazed into her eyes a moment longer and then his lips swooped down on hers in a kiss that fairly swept her breath away. At the same time, his hands went to work removing her clothing and she eagerly moved her body first one way and then the other to aid him in the task.

After he'd finally peeled away the last scrap of her underwear, he stood to one side of the bed to shed his jeans and boots. As she watched his long, lean body emerge in the dim light, her heart began to pound with anticipation. And when he returned to her, she reached for him without hesitation.

"I'd planned on letting you sleep by yourself tonight,"

he said, his voice hoarse with desire. His hands cupped both breasts and his head bent so that his mouth could make a wet foray over one nipple. "I thought you'd want it that way."

"You thought wrong. Very wrong." Her arms wrapped around him, her legs threaded through his. "Thank you for giving me a wedding night, Liam."

"My absolute pleasure, Kit."

After that there was no further need for words. Nor was there time for talking. Kitty was too busy using her hands and lips to explore his hard body and too consumed with desire to be able to utter more than soft sighs of pleasure.

And when he finally entered her, she was so choked with emotion that tears stung her eyes and the faint moan trapped in her throat was more like a whimper than anything else.

The sound prompted him to pause and glance down at her.

"Kitty? Am I hurting you?"

"No! Just love me, Liam! Love me!" she implored.

Her plea was all he needed to urge him on and he didn't hold back as her hips arched toward his. With a needy groan he drove into her then moved into a rhythm that set Kitty's senses swirling into a raging fire. In a matter of moments she was moving frantically against him, seeking and straining for more and more of the incredible pleasure he was giving.

Somewhere in the back of her fevered mind, she was partially aware of his hands racing over her body, the sweat trickling off his skin and onto hers. In the silence of the room she could hear the rapid intake of his breath followed by her own. And in her ears, the pounding of her heart was like a deep bass, throbbing to the frantic pace of their bodies.

She didn't know how much time had passed or what finally pushed her to the brink. All she knew was that she was suddenly flying...soaring among the stars and clouds then drifting ever so slowly back to the warm, sweet circle of her husband's arms.

The next morning when the alarm buzzed loudly next to Liam's head, he groggily punched the off button then turned over to see that Kitty's side of the bed was empty.

Although it shouldn't have, the sight chilled him. He wasn't sure what he'd been expecting from his wife this morning. Maybe a kiss or a smile. At the very least, he'd expected her to be lying next to him.

Don't be a sap, Liam. Kitty gave you a night of great sex. And that's all you gave her. If you're looking for bells and whistles and coffee in bed, you're in for a disappointment.

Disgusted with the mocking voice in his head, he threw back the covers and quickly headed to the shower. By the time he dressed and arrived in the kitchen, he found Kitty standing at the cabinet counter, washing down a piece of toast with a cup of decaffeinated coffee.

Seeing she was already dressed for work, he glanced at his watch. It was only a quarter after five, but that was a late hour for a trainer. "Good morning," he greeted.

Placing her cup on its saucer, she turned her head to look at him. "Good morning."

Although there wasn't a smile on her face, the softness to her features took away some of the sting of finding himself alone in their bed.

"You're up early. Headed to the track?" he asked.

She nodded. "I have two fillies scheduled for early workouts this morning. I need to be there. Clayton is developing a good eye, but he doesn't always pick up on the little nuances."

She dabbed a napkin to her lips and as she turned to toss the paper into a trash bin, Liam couldn't help but notice how fetching she looked in a pair of jeans and thin yellow sweater. Her honey-blond hair was swept back from her face with a blue paisley scarf and the deep color made her blue eyes even more vivid.

Walking over to the cabinet, he took down a cup and filled it with coffee. "Did you find everything here in the kitchen? If there's anything else you want or need I'll send the girls out for it."

"I woke a little later than usual this morning. Other than make a pot of this decaf coffee and a piece of toast, I've not had time to really look things over." She looked at him, her expression curious. "Do you normally eat breakfast? I didn't think to ask. If you'd like to eat now, I could try to fix something."

He chuckled. "Kitty, I don't expect you to act like a proper little wife with an apron wrapped around your waist and a spoon and spatula in your hands."

She looked away from him but not before he saw a slight frown crease her forehead. As he sipped the strong coffee, he wondered what could be going through her head. Last night she'd been so giving, so loving in his arms. Now she seemed more like an acquaintance than his wife.

"I didn't plan on becoming a 'proper' little wife," she said flatly. "I was trying to be gracious."

It was clear he'd said the wrong thing. But damn it, he didn't want her thinking she'd suddenly become his slave just because they'd signed a marriage certificate.

Biting back a sigh, he walked over to where she was standing. "Sorry, Kitty. I just wanted you to understand that I'm used to doing for myself. But I do thank you for the offer anyway. It was nice of you."

In other words he didn't need or want a wife fussing over his personal needs, Kitty thought. The fact should have filled her with relief. She didn't have time to coddle a demanding husband. But it would be nice to think she was needed for more than sex and a bearer of his baby.

Quickly, before he could spot her disappointment, she walked around him and plucked up a shoulder bag from the kitchen table. "I've got to be going."

She was almost out the door when he caught her arm from behind. Her brows arched in question, she turned back to him.

"If you'll give me five minutes I'll drive the both of us to the track," he offered.

"That isn't necessary. I'm used to doing for myself," she stiffly repeated the words he'd given her.

Shaking his head with frustration, he said, "I think we should start this morning over again, Kit."

His low, rough voice pulled on her senses and before she could stop them, memories of the night before began to swamp her thoughts. The touch of his hands and taste of his lips had worked magic on her senses. His body had driven her to paradise and back again. And with each minute that had passed in his arms, she'd fallen in love just that much more.

But once their bodies had parted and cooled, she'd felt an invisible something creep between them. Instead of cradling her in his arms and telling her what their love-making had meant to him, he'd suggested she go to sleep and rest, then swiftly turned away from her.

"Why should we do that?" she asked.

With a wry smile, he gathered her into his arms and

pulled her close. "This is our first full day of being husband and wife. We don't want to start it out with a quarrel."

"We're not quarreling," she said breathlessly as her heart drummed against his hard chest. "We're learning about each other."

"Hmm. Well, I think there's a much more pleasant way to learn about each other, don't you?"

Mesmerized, she watched his face dip closer and then his lips were moving against hers, creating a heaven she couldn't resist.

She shouldn't be so weak, she thought, so pitifully attracted to him. But she couldn't stop the thrill rushing through her body any more than she could push aside the love he instilled in her heart.

Easing his lips slightly back from hers, he murmured, "You could call Clayton and tell him you'll be a little late, couldn't you?"

To do such a thing would wreck her morning schedule, she realized desperately. But to turn away from her husband would wreck it even more.

After a moment's hesitation, she eased out of his arms and pulled her phone from her bag. Once she'd exchanged a few brief words with her assistant, she turned back to Liam, and as he led her down the hallway to their bedroom, she wondered how long it would be before she woke up from this fog of desire? How long would it be before she realized that loving this man was going to take away everything she'd ever wanted in her life?

Chapter Seven

Later that morning, behind the training barn, Kitty stood watching the groom wash down Black Dahlia, a three-year-old filly that she and her father had coddled since she was a baby. Will had predicted big things from the horse and Kitty had sworn to do her damnedest to make sure Dahlia excelled to the winner's circle. Everything Kitty had ever wanted depended on the filly's success.

But the hot steam rising from Dahlia's back couldn't begin to compare with the heated fury Kitty was lashing on her assistant.

"I don't know what in hell you thought you were doing, Clayton! I told you to work this filly for no more than four furlongs. And I damned well didn't want her opened up at this late stage of the game! She runs in seven days! Or have you forgotten that, too?"

Clayton stared at her, his expression stiff. "I don't know why you're raking me over the coals about this. Rodrigo is the one who worked her. And I'd assumed you'd already given him orders for this morning."

Kitty heaved out a heavy breath as she tried to compose herself. It wasn't like her to lose her temper. In fact, she couldn't remember a time she'd ever yelled at Clayton or any of her staff. But this was a whopping mistake, one that might cost them all dearly.

"I did give him orders. But his English is sometimes spotty. That's why I wanted you to go over everything with him in Spanish this morning!"

A muscle jumped in Clayton's tight jaw. "I did. I told him to follow your instructions. Besides, I had other things to do. It's not like I was sitting around on my hands waiting for you to get here."

His comment hit home and her cheeks burned as she looked away from him. Instead of taking care of business, she'd been making love to Liam. Clayton didn't know that, but he was probably thinking it and that was just as bad. To him it didn't matter that she'd only gotten married yesterday. Being late this morning made her look indifferent and irresponsible, especially since a training mistake had been made.

"Don't worry. It won't happen again," she said tightly.

Muttering a curse, Clayton lifted his cowboy hat from his head and slammed fingers through his thick hair. "Damn it, Kitty, I don't know why you're so fired up about this. Dahlia worked a bullet! You should be happy to learn she has that much speed."

A bullet meant the fastest workout for any horse of the morning going at the same distance. That was impressive. But it was also worrisome to Kitty. "Look, Clayton, I don't have the advantage of years of training experience like my father had. And you have even more to learn than

I do," she said tersely. "Each horse is different and they have to be trained accordingly."

"I know that," he shot back at her. "This isn't my first day at the track. So don't start treating me like it is!"

"Dahlia is small and delicate. God only knows what this work is going to take out of her. I can only hope and pray she'll recuperate before she runs next week." Turning, she started to head back to the barn, but stopped to fling one last thing at him. "Do not put this filly back into her stall until she's completely dry and cool to the touch! Think you can handle that?"

"Yes, ma'am!"

He gave her a mocking salute and Kitty swiveled on the heel of her boot and stalked into the barn. She was striding quickly down the shed row toward her office when her cell rang. Once she'd arrived at the track this morning, the calls had been practically incessant. She'd answered only the most urgent ones and let her voice mail pick up the rest. Since she was in no mood to talk to anyone at the moment, she didn't bother to pull the instrument from her jeans pocket and glance at the caller ID number.

By the time she was seated behind her desk, the alert of an incoming message sounded on her phone, so she swiped it on and quickly listened to the voice at the other end. Even if she wasn't in the mood for conversation, she didn't want to irk an owner. The last thing she needed was for the barn to lose horses just because she didn't make herself available.

But to her surprise it wasn't an owner. The caller had been a sportswriter for the DRF, who was interested in doing an article on her. The focus of the story would be on Kitty becoming the main trainer for Desert End and how she was coping on her own now that Will was gone.

Once the message ended, Kitty put the phone aside and

with a heavy sigh, dropped her head in her hands. What would her father be thinking of her now? she wondered miserably. He was a man who'd wanted and expected his orders to be followed to the letter. Yet if someone made a mistake he hadn't lost his cool as she'd just done with Clayton.

Her father had never been nearly seven months pregnant, either, she thought crossly. But that was no excuse. He'd had his share of problems and for the most part he'd dealt with them in a dignified manner. She had to do the same.

Trying to push the whole episode out of her mind, she plucked up a workout sheet from her desktop and tried to focus on the fraction splits and track conditions. But her mind continued to jump in all directions. It was almost a relief when a knock sounded on the door and Clayton stuck his head around the edge of the wooden panel.

"May I come in?"

Leaning back in her chair, she motioned for him to enter the office. "I'm glad you're here," she said dully. "I need to apologize to you."

He stepped into the room and shut the door behind him. "There's no need for that. I'm the one who was out of line. I should have made sure Rodrigo understood exactly what to do with Dahlia. When you're not here, I'm in charge, so it was my responsibility and I let you down."

Shaking her head, she said, "Forget it." She blew out a long breath and glanced away from him. "I should have been here."

His features taut with concern, he moved to the front of Kitty's desk and stared down at her. "No. You shouldn't be here at all, Kitty. And frankly, I don't get it. You just got married yesterday. When you told me you'd be here this morning, I was shocked. I thought newlyweds wanted to be alone. If I had a wife who looked like you I damned sure wouldn't be at the track the day after my wedding."

No. She supposed Clayton would treat a new wife differently. But then she seriously doubted he would ever marry, unless he was head over heels in love. He was the romantic sort. Not a practical man like Liam.

Blushing, she looked at him. "You like the way a pregnant woman looks?"

His gaze didn't waver. "It looks good on you."

Feeling uncomfortable now, she said, "Well, there's more to things than what you see, Clayton. Liam and I will take a honeymoon when the time is right."

Jamming his hands in the front pockets of his jeans, he looked down at the floor. "You know, when I first learned you were going to have a baby I tried to guess who the father might be. Liam Donovan never came into the picture, Kitty. Not even once."

He obviously has a thing for you. At the time Liam had made the remark about Clayton, she'd totally dismissed it. But now she wondered if her assistant had harbored feelings about her at one time or another. Dear God, she hoped not. She knew firsthand how terrible it was to love someone and not have that person love you in return.

Clearing her throat, she said, "I imagine there're plenty of people around here who were just as surprised as you. Liam was a widower for a long time."

He lifted his head and for a moment he looked as though he was going to say more on the matter, but he must have decided he'd said enough because he gave her a wan grin. "I'd better get back to work. The blacksmith is coming in a few minutes to reset Mr. Marvel's shoes. I want to be there."

She nodded, and he headed for the door. As he started

to leave, he glanced over his shoulder at her. "I'm sorry about Dahlia."

Kitty bit back a sigh. "And I'm sorry I lost my temper. So let's just call it even, okay?"

"Okay."

Clayton shut the door behind him and Kitty had to fight to keep a wall of tears from clouding her eyes.

Pretend. Make believe. Sham. That's all her life seemed to be now. One act rolling into another. First their families and friends, now the people she worked with. They all needed to believe that she was happy, her marriage perfect.

When Liam had first suggested they put on an act, something deep and instinctive had told her it would be a mistake…that problems would surely arise from trying to create a false illusion. But in the end she'd agreed with him because he was a very persuasive man and because it was much, much easier on her pride to let people believe that Liam loved her, that they conceived this baby out of that passionate love.

She'd never dreamed that all the pretending would leave her feeling so drained and empty. She was beginning to feel like a habitual liar and she wondered how much longer she could continue to convincingly play the part.

Later that afternoon, after a lunch of chicken salad and a carton of milk, Kitty left the confines of her office carrying a manila envelope full of important papers she needed to present to the secretary in the racing office, which was located in a separate building at the far end of the stable area.

Since they'd parted early this morning, she'd not seen Liam. But he'd informed her that he'd be tied up with workouts and later, meetings with a blood stock buyer and a couple of jockey agents. Now, as she passed the stalls where his horses were housed, she could see his staff was still very busy walking, grooming and generally making sure that each animal was happy.

"Oh, that feels good doesn't it, sweetheart? Yes, I can see just how beautiful you are, but I can't keep doing this forever. No matter how much you like it."

The sound of Liam's voice suddenly caught her attention and she glanced to her left and the stall where it seemed to have originated. From where she stood, she couldn't see around the filled hay bag hanging at the side of the door, so she walked over to the half gate and peered inside.

What she saw brought an immediate smile to her face. Liam and a chestnut filly were having a playful interaction as he made a game of massaging her gums.

"If my teeth were that beautiful I'd be laughing all the time," he told the horse as his fingers caught the horse's lips and jiggled them up and down in the simulation of a laugh.

Kitty chuckled. "She's saying she does laugh. She just doesn't let you know when she's doing it."

At the sound of her voice, Liam instantly looked over his shoulder to see her stepping into the stall.

"Kitty. I didn't know you were there."

The smile remained on her face as she went to stand beside him and the filly. "And I didn't know I had female competition. Who is this beautiful young lady, anyway? Aren't you going to introduce us?"

"This is Royal Daisy," he said proudly. "She's two years old and I'm heading her toward the Del Mar Futurity later this year."

"Oh. Well, it sounds like you have royal ambitions for this classy lady."

Easing up to the filly, Kitty ran a hand over Daisy's

back and onto her hips. Beneath the shiny red coat was a faint pattern of dapples, a certain sign of her excellent health. Liam was known for being a trainer who built his horses from the inside out and she'd always admired him greatly for not only winning races, but also for the infinite care he gave each runner.

"So you plan on racing at Del Mar, too?" she asked offhandedly, even though she was anxious to learn his intentions. The Del Mar meet would begin shortly after the baby was due. At that time, she wanted to be back in Texas, where Coral, the longtime Desert End housekeeper, would be ready to help her. The woman had raised seven children in her lifetime. If anyone knew about babies and their needs, it was her.

He looked at her keenly. "That's been my plan all along. Why? Are you going to ship your horses down there, too?"

What was the man thinking, besides the next race he was going to enter? she wondered, as she tried not to become vexed with him. "I've not planned that far ahead yet. Besides, the first few weeks of Del Mar will be up to Clayton. Since I'll be indisposed at that time."

A puzzled frown marred his forehead. "Indisposed? What—" His gaze fell to her belly. "Oh. The baby will be coming in the first week or so of July. Well, that alters things a bit."

"Just a bit," she said drily, then stepping around him, she started out of the stall.

He turned away from the filly and started after her. "Kitty, wait! Are you leaving angry?"

Angry? After this morning and the round she'd had with Clayton, she was going to try to keep anger off the radar of her emotions. But that still left disappointment and right at this moment she was feeling the weight of it.

"No." Trying her best to smile, she held up the manila

envelope she was carrying. "I need to go to the racing office with these papers."

His hand rested on her shoulder and suddenly her mind
was swamped with memories of this morning when he'd
carried her back to bed, the way he'd gently undressed her,
the way his eyes had closed when he'd sought her lips and
how his hands had skimmed over her skin, leaving goose
bumps in their wake.

"You're thinking I'm a selfish bastard. I can see it on
your face."

No, she thought, he was seeing a woman that was
swiftly losing her grip. "That's an awful thing to say,"
she said.

His nostrils flared slightly as his fingers moved away
from her shoulder to curve against her neck. "If I sound
like a jerk it's because it's been a long time since I've had
anyone other than myself to consider. Give me a chance,
Kit, and I promise to do better."

Yes, she supposed the years he'd been without his wife
had turned him into a solitary man and perhaps he'd forgotten how to share things with a woman. She could forgive him those things. Besides, he'd called her Kit and
the way he'd said it so soft and raspy had melted everything inside her.

"I've already forgotten the whole thing," she told him.

His features softened. "Good. Because it doesn't matter what race or horse or track is happening at the time
you go into labor. When this baby decides to be born, I'll
be with you."

Yes, physically he'd be with her. She had no doubt about
that. But emotionally would he be holding her hand and
wishing she was the woman he'd lost, the woman he had
really loved?

When Kitty had first met Liam, he'd still been married, but she'd never met his wife during that time. In fact, Kitty had never seen the woman at any of the tracks where the Donovans and Cartwrights had raced in the past. She could only assume that Felicia hadn't been that involved in her husband's work. But he'd obviously adored his late wife. All these years since her death, he'd never shown any interest in another woman. And the only interest he'd directed at Kitty had been physical, not emotional. That had to mean his heart was still connected to his late wife.

But she wasn't going to think about that now, she told herself. A few weeks ago, she'd not pictured Liam being with her in any capacity, other than to hand their child back and forth between custodial visits. The fact that he'd married her was still a bit overwhelming to Kitty and she realized that, for now, she had to be satisfied with the part of him he was willing to give. And perhaps, if she was lucky, he might someday decide to give her his heart.

By the time the weekend arrived April had rolled into the month of May. Liam was growing more accustomed to the idea of having a wife again. At least, in a general sense. Having a woman in his house, his bed and his future was becoming a fixture in his thoughts. Whenever he made plans now, he didn't just make them for himself, he had to include Kitty. He had to consider her condition, her wishes and thoughts. And though the changes in his daily habits had been abrupt and drastic, he realized he'd never felt so renewed or energized. Had Kitty done all that to him? Or the coming baby?

Four weeks ago, he would have been quick to answer that self-imposed question. At that time, his baby had been the driving force behind every decision he'd made. It was all that had mattered to him. But that was beginning to change and that was the only thing that kept his life from being idyllic. Loving the baby was a natural response. It was his child, created from a part of him. He'd be a worthless man if he didn't love it.

But falling in love with Kitty? No! He didn't want to think that might be happening. All those memories of Felicia were still crowding his mind, reminding him over and over of how it felt to love and lose. Her death and that of his child had brought him years of loneliness and guilt, confusion, sorrow and bitterness. And he'd spent just as many years trying to keep all those emotions bottled inside, trying to pretend to everyone, especially his family, that he'd moved on and was living life to the fullest again.

No, he thought again, as the roar of the crowd could be heard rising up from the grandstand on the main track. He might enjoy Kitty's company as they shared the same home and the same jobs; enjoy being married to her and having sex with her. But he wasn't going to love her. That was too risky a venture and one that he wasn't willing to take.

Shoving that thought away, he glanced down at his watch then back to the horse Andy was leading around the walking ring. He and the valet had already saddled the brown colt called Awesome Joe. The blue saddle towel depicting the number 3 was smooth upon the animal's back, the girth tight around his chest, the shadow roll on his nose in the perfect spot.

As Liam went through the mental checklist, the jockey strode up to him and thrust out his hand.

"Good afternoon, Mr. Donovan. Thanks for giving me the opportunity to ride Joe for you and his owner, J and M Stables."

Smiling, Liam shook the rider's hand. He'd known Michael O'Day for several years and had used him here on the West Coast on many of his runners. He always called him Mike, but the jockey still insisted on calling Liam by his surname.

"I'm glad you're going to be aboard," Liam assured him. "How's the wife? The family?"

After a few polite exchanges that had nothing to do with racing, Mike brought the conversation back around. "Any special instructions today?" he asked.

"No. He's feeling good," Liam told him. "And you've been on him before. You know he's a closer. Just do your thing and hopefully he'll do his."

The jockey nodded. "Looks like the nine will give us plenty of speed to run to today."

"Yeah," Liam agreed. "Just get Joe to relax and I think he'll give you a good trip home."

At that moment the paddock judge yelled out, "Riders up!"

Following the cue, Liam legged the jockey upon Awesome Joe's back, and the colt began to dance in anticipation of the job he had ahead of him. Andy took a firm hold of the lead rein and headed the horse and rider toward the tunnel that would take him beneath the stadium and onto the main track and the waiting pony horse.

Once they were on their way, Liam hurried to the grandstand and the box seats that had been allotted to him. He found Kitty already there and his eyes very nearly popped at the sight of her.

A white sundress splashed with bright exotic flowers draped across her breasts in tiny pleats, while the whole garment was held up by skinny straps over her shoulders. A tiny headband with a cluster of wispy feathers that matched her dress adorned her long blond hair, while diamonds dangled from her ears.

Her pink lips smiled impishly at his wide eyes. "What's

wrong? Didn't recognize me in a dress without the smell of hay and horse liniment?"

For most of this week, he'd either seen her wearing jeans, boots and a big work shirt at the stable area, or nothing at all in his bed. To see her so polished and elegant was quite a switch.

Chuckling softly, he bent and placed a kiss on her smooth temple. The scent of flowers and grass and the ocean drifted to his nostrils. "You look beautiful. And I don't smell a hint of horse liniment," he teased.

"Well, I realize Thursday was opening day and this is Saturday, but I wanted to dress for the occasion anyway. If your Awesome Joe runs like you tell me he will, we might just get to pose for a win picture."

"Let's hope."

There were a myriad of things that could go wrong in a race. But right now, Liam didn't want to think about any of them. He always got as nervous as hell right before any of his horses ran and today, with his beautiful wife looking on, he especially wanted things to go right.

Go right! You want more than that—you want to win, Liam! You want to impress Kitty. Show her that you're good at your job. That you're a man she can be proud of.

The little voice in his head sounded like a teenager wanting to impress his first date and the idea that he'd gone that sappy had him groaning out loud.

Kitty looked at him and then, as though she understood his nerves were in upheaval, she reached over and clasped his hand in hers.

"Don't worry. You've done your job. It's out of your hands now."

She really did understand, he thought. But that shouldn't amaze him. She'd grown up in this business. She'd dealt with the fears and worries, the highs and lows that went

with the job. But then, his late wife had also been familiar with the horse-racing industry, too. After all, they'd
been married for nearly five years. And though Felicia
hadn't necessarily shared his passion for the sport, she'd
supported his endeavors. Yet his late wife had never understood exactly what it all meant to him; how everything about it, from seeing the foals born to standing in
the winner's circle, to finding dignified jobs for the retired thoroughbreds coursed through his blood. The fact
that Kitty did understand pulled on his emotions, and in
a strange way, left him feeling guilty. Felicia had been a
wonderful wife to him. She'd been his first and only love.
He'd be a traitor to let Kitty come in and fill up his heart.
Or would he?

The post parade was making its way in front of the
grandstand and though he tried to focus on the field of
runners and how they were behaving, he was completely
distracted by the feel of Kitty's little hand wrapped around
his and how much her words had comforted him.

*Watch out, Liam. If you don't catch yourself you're
going to stumble around and fall in love.*

As soon as the thought tumbled through his mind, he
pulled his hand away from Kitty's and lifted a pair of binoculars to his eyes.

Love. This was a hell of a time to let that word enter
his mind. They were in a grandstand filled with specta-
tors. He had a high-class colt starting for the first time
as a three-year-old. The owners were expecting Liam to
produce great things from the horse. These were anxious
moments for a trainer.

Yet in spite of all these worries and distractions, he
couldn't forget or ignore Kitty's presence beside him. And
though he was watching the progress of the horses with
the aid of the binoculars, the image of Kitty's lovely face

framed by blond hair and a sassy sprout of feathers swam through his mind.

"The track is in perfect condition today," she commented. "And the three hole ought to be good for Joe. Mike can hold him midpack, along the rail, and save ground."

"Yeah. Or get boxed in," he muttered.

"Losing is a part of the game, Liam."

Losing was a part of life, too, he wanted to tell her. A piece of the pie that he never wanted to taste again.

Lowering the binoculars, he looked down to see she had her gaze on him instead of the starting gate.

Liam swallowed hard. His wife. His baby. This time he was going to do everything in his power to hold on to his family. To lose them would end him. It was that simple and that frightening.

"Not this time, Kitty."

Chapter Eight

Was he talking about the baby? Her? Or the race? Even if Kitty had wanted to ask, she didn't have an opportunity as the starting gates suddenly popped and the twelve-horse field burst onto the track.

As she watched Awesome Joe settle into a long, rhythmic stride back in the middle of the pack, she sent up a silent prayer for the horse and rider. It didn't quite make sense, but she wanted this win for Liam more than she'd ever wanted one for herself. And as the horses passed the half-mile marker, she watched, scarcely breathing, as Joe began to make a slight move along the rail.

"He's moving," Liam said, the binoculars still glued to his face.

Preferring to watch with her naked eye, Kitty replied, "I see. He looks comfortable. And happy."

"Yeah. His ears are pricked."

By now it was only two furlongs to the finish line. The

jockey shook the reins at Joe and the colt shot forward as though he had rockets on his hooves. Unfortunately, so did the eight horse on the outside.

"Come on, Joe! Dig down, boy! Come on! Come on! You got him!" Kitty yelled while bouncing on her toes.

Side by side, heads bobbing, the pair of horses battled it out to the wire. Once they passed it, the crowd was roaring and Kitty and Liam exchanged questioning looks.

"What do you think?" Kitty asked hopefully.

He let out a choked laugh. "From this angle it was way too close to say! Come on, let's make our way down."

He grabbed her hand and while they worked their way through the crowd, the photo sign flashed on the tote board and the announcer was instructing everyone to hold all wagering tickets. Out on the track Andy was leading Joe and rider around in a circle while nearby the eight and his groom and rider were doing the same.

Three. Eight. Five. Ten. When the numbers finally lit up the board, the crowd roared, Liam grabbed Kitty by the shoulders and kissed her soundly on the mouth.

"Let's go get our picture taken, Mrs. Donovan," he said with a happy laugh.

When Kitty and Liam finally returned home later that night, she was exhausted, but happier than she'd ever been since the two of them had married.

She wasn't sure what was going on in Liam's head. If Joe winning the photo finish had put him in a joyous mood, or if something deep within him was changing. Either way, the whole day had turned fairy tale for her.

At the track, he'd kept her close to his side and if he'd not had his arm around her waist, he'd been clasping her arm or hand or shoulder as if touching her and having her close was as natural as breathing to him. And after the races had ended, he'd taken her to an elegant nightspot for their dinner and for the first time ever she'd danced in her husband's arms.

Now as they entered the house, she didn't want the night to end and her sigh must have spoken volumes as he'd turned and locked the door behind them.

"Tired?" he asked.

"Mmm. A little," she admitted as she stretched her arms above her head. "But today was so nice it was all worth it."

Leaving the door, he snaked an arm around her shoulders and urged her out of the foyer and through the living room.

"Why don't you go on to the bedroom," he suggested, "and I'll bring you a glass of milk or juice. Whatever you'd like."

"I'd like real coffee with caffeine. Doused with gobs of cream and sugar," she said with wry humor. "But I'll settle for milk."

He chuckled as he broke away from her side and headed toward an arched doorway that would eventually lead him to the kitchen. "Our child will thank you for it whenever he goes for dental checkups."

Up until today, nearly all Liam's thoughts and actions toward Kitty pertained to the baby and its welfare. She could understand that up to a point and she certainly didn't want to be a woman that was jealous or resentful of her own child. But tonight, when he'd danced with her, she'd wanted to think it was all for her and no one else. And that had made her feel like a woman; a woman that was needed for more than just a sex partner or a baby incubator.

In the bedroom, she slipped off her clothes and pulled on a blue satin robe that fell to her knees. Since the wrapped garment was supposed to belt at the waist, she tied the sash just beneath her breasts, which along with her belly, had grown considerably since she'd arrived in California a little more than a month ago.

She'd always had a slender build, and even now, she'd managed to maintain the weight gain her doctor had prescribed. Yet as she caught her reflection in the dresser mirror, she realized it wouldn't be long until her size grew cumbersome, making her job at the barn that much harder.

But she refused to dwell on that worrisome fact tonight as she pressed the satin over her protruding belly and gazed thoughtfully at her reflection. She was having Liam's child and that made every little ache and discomfort of her pregnancy worth it.

"The baby is growing."

At the sound of Liam's voice, she turned to see him walking toward her, a small glass of milk in his hand. Smiling, she accepted the drink.

"Along with me. I'm heading toward my eighth month." While she sipped the milk, he removed his tie and shrugged out of his pale blue dress shirt. As he draped the garments over the back of a chair, she went on, "Actually I should tell you that I have a checkup with my doctor next Wednesday. He'll tell me then if I'm growing too much."

He tossed a questioning glance at her. "You're keeping your doctor in El Paso?"

She nodded, a bit mystified that this was a matter they'd not yet discussed. But their days were consumed with their jobs and when they were alone together, they didn't do a whole lot of talking.

"Yes. At this stage in my pregnancy I hate to change physicians."

"I understand. But that's going to be inconvenient, isn't it? Especially since we'll still be here in California when the baby arrives."

Shrugging, she placed the empty glass on one of the nightstands that flanked the bed. "It's a short flight from here to there. And when my due date grows near I'll stay on the ranch."

Frowning, he walked over to where she stood. "But that's not where you're living now."

"No. But Desert End is my home."

A pause of silence followed her statement, causing her to take a second glance at him.

"If that's your home, then what is this place?" he finally asked.

"It's where I'm living for now," she reasoned. "But it's not my home. My home is Desert End. Just like the Diamond D is yours."

"I didn't realize you felt that way. That first night we were married you called it home."

He sounded hurt, almost resentful, and she arched her brows at him. "That was just a figure of speech. Why? Is something wrong with the way I feel?"

He turned away from her and she watched him take a seat on the edge of the bed. As he pulled off his boots, he said in a flat voice, "No. I guess I was a little confused about things. Or I guess you'd call it a little old-fashioned. I thought wherever a man and wife lived together was their home."

Her hand pressed against the side of her belly as a hollow feeling struck the middle of her chest. *Home is where the heart is.* She wanted to repeat the old adage to him, but she didn't. Because Kitty wasn't in his heart. Not the way she wanted to be. But what did she expect? He'd told her straight out that after he'd lost his wife he'd not ever planned or wanted to marry again. Clearly, Felicia had been his one and only love. There wasn't room in his heart for Kitty, too.

But maybe that could change, she dared to think. Today at the races he'd felt so close to her and tonight as she'd danced in his arms, sparks of hope had lifted her spirits.

She moved closer until she was standing next to his knee. "Liam," she said softly, "we've been living here for less than a month. That's not long enough to make it feel like home yet." She touched his bare shoulder. "And you're not old-fashioned. Not to me."

He looked up at her and something glimmered in his eyes. She couldn't define the emotion, but whatever it was drew her to him, made her ache to hold him close.

"Kit."

Her name came out as a whisper and she lowered her face to his and pressed her lips to his forehead before moving on to his cheeks and chin and finally his mouth.

As his lips quickly possessed hers, he eased her down on the bed, until her back was resting against the mattress. Wrapping her arms around him, she urged him closer, while her lips parted to allow his tongue to plunge deep within her mouth.

A rush of sensations immediately consumed her, causing her fingers to curl into his back, a moan to sound deep in her throat. He left her senseless, she thought, a puppet that only he could bring to life with his kisses, his touches.

When he finally eased his mouth back from hers, she was already drunk with desire and hungry for more.

"You should be resting," he murmured.

"I am resting," she purred. "Here in your arms."

"We've had a long, tiring day."

Curling her arm around his neck, she made sure his head didn't move away from hers. "And it's been so lovely. I don't want it to end," she added.

Gazing into her eyes, he thrust his fingers into her long hair and stroked it ever so gently away from her face. "I don't know what you do to me, Kit. But whatever it is isn't normal. No man should want a woman the way I want you."

Want. It wasn't the same as love. But for the moment it was enough to make her smile.

She said, "You almost make it sound like a sickness."

Groaning, he brought his lips next to hers. "I think it is. Can you cure me?"

Sighing with pleasure, she closed her eyes and found his lips.

Two days later, on Tuesday evening, she was entering Mr. Marvel's stall when Clayton caught up to her.

"Kitty, do you have a minute? I need to talk with you," he said.

"Sure. I'm listening." She motioned for him to follow her into the stall. "I'm just making my last rounds before Liam and I quit for the day. Is anything wrong," she asked.

He let out a heavy sigh and Kitty glanced over her shoulder to see him wiping a hand over his face.

"I just got off the phone," he explained. "Dad had to go to the hospital this afternoon with chest pains. Now Mom tells me he's scheduled for surgery early in the morning."

Concerned, she turned away from the horse to give him her complete attention. Although she didn't know Clayton's parents all that well, she'd met them a few times and considered them friends. "That quickly? It must be serious."

"Blockage. They may try a stent, but it could turn into open heart surgery. The doctors aren't sure yet." He grimaced. "I feel like I should be there, Kitty. I know you need me here—especially since—well, you can't stay on the run in your condition. But—"

"You don't need to say anything, Clayton. Your father's

health is the most important thing right now. Your mother needs you there to support her. I insist that you go!"

He shook his head and she could see the whole matter was weighing heavily on him.

"I have no idea how long I might have to be gone," he admitted.

"Don't worry about it," she assured him, then smiled. "I'll manage. Promise."

"Maybe Bella should fly out and help you. I realize she's busy at the ranch, but you'll need—"

Bella was the assistant trainer, who was keeping everything going back at Desert End. To have her here would be a huge help to Kitty, but her presence at the ranch was even more important.

"I need her at the ranch. The horses there are just as important. You know that."

"Damn it, you need another trainer, Kitty. When are you going to break down and hire someone? Now is the time—while you're pregnant and need the extra help!"

Now was not the time, she thought desperately. Clayton didn't know it, but there was too much uncertainty in Kitty's life to bring another person into the picture. And none of it had anything to do with her marriage to Liam. Too much hinged on the Oaks and how Dahlia preformed. If she failed, everything would be up for grabs, including her home and her livelihood.

"It's not possible, Clayton. Maybe in the future. If the barn keeps winning."

Flabbergasted, he stared at her. "If! Kitty—"

"Clayton, you need to be going," she interrupted sharply. "So go. The grooms will deal with the heavy tasks. Besides, Liam will lend a helping hand, if need be."

Only Kitty hoped she didn't have to ask for Liam's help. Like Owen had said, once he learned of the predicament

her father had left her in, Liam might think differently of
her and her reason for accepting his marriage proposal.
He might think she'd married him because he was a successful trainer and not because they were having a child
together. But she couldn't let herself worry about that at
the moment. She already had so many worries they were
about to crush her.

Clayton remained skeptical. "I don't like doing this,
Kitty. But I really have no choice."

"That's right. You don't." She latched on to his arm and
urged him out of the stall.

While he fastened the gate behind them, he said glumly,
"My flight is leaving in a couple of hours. I'd better be
going."

She asked, "Do you need a ride to the airport?"

"No. I'll drive." He turned to face her, his expression
torn. "I'll call or text as soon as I get any news about Dad."

"I'll be praying for him."

"Thanks, Kitty."

Bending his head, he placed a kiss on her cheek. She
did her best to smile as she waved him off. But as she
turned back to Mr. Marvel's stall, she had to fight to keep
from laying her head against the cinderblock wall and
weeping.

For the past several months, since her father had died,
she'd relied heavily on Clayton. Especially when her grief
over losing Will had been so deep, she'd struggled just to
get out of bed. Now the days were ticking down. The baby
was coming and so was the race of her life.

"Is something going on that I need to know about?"

The sound of Liam's voice was directly behind her
and she turned to see he'd walked up without her even
knowing it.

"Clayton is leaving," she said bluntly.

One of his brows arched mockingly. "The man kisses you whenever he leaves the barn in the evenings?"

Kitty stared at him. Could he actually be jealous? No, she quickly decided. A man had to be crazy about a woman before he could be jealous of her.

"No, he was kissing me goodbye. He's leaving California and flying back to Texas tonight."

Liam moved closer and Kitty desperately wanted to fling herself into his arms and sob against his chest. But she couldn't break apart in front of her husband. He wouldn't understand such an emotional outburst and trying to explain her predicament would only make matters worse.

A concerned frown suddenly puckered his features. "Oh? Is anything wrong at Desert End?"

Kitty shook her head. "It's Clayton's father. He's been hospitalized and scheduled for heart surgery in the morning. He hates to leave. He's afraid I won't have enough help."

"I hope you reminded him that you have a husband who knows a thing or two about horses. I'm here to help whenever you need me."

With a grateful little smile, she stepped forward and wrapped her arms around his neck. It was a relief when his arms came around her and pulled her tight against him.

"Thank you, Liam," she murmured, her cheek pressed against his shoulder. "Very much."

His hand smoothed a long trail down her back. "You are still keeping your doctor's appointment, aren't you? I don't want you to cancel it just because your assistant isn't here to take care of things."

She lifted her head to look at him. "I didn't tell Clayton that I was flying back tomorrow to see the doctor. He already had enough worries about his father. But yes—I still

intend to go. My grooms can handle things for a couple
of days. My only concern is that Mr. Marvel is scheduled
to work before I get back. If you could watch him. And
Black Dahlia is scheduled for the Grade II on Sunday. It's
imperative that everything stay on course for her. She has
to do well in this, Liam. Otherwise, the Oaks—"

The sound of approaching voices had them automati-
cally ending the embrace, but Liam kept his hand firmly
on her arm as the group of workers passed them by.

"I understand how important Dahlia is to you," he said,
"but I was thinking that I should go with you for the doctor's visit."

Liam couldn't possibly understand just what Dahlia
meant to her and every person working at Desert End,
she thought. But his suggestion of accompanying her to El
Paso was enough to push the filly from her mind for the
moment and she studied him with a measure of surprise.

Was this show of concern for the baby's health or
hers? His motive shouldn't matter, she told herself. Yet
she wanted to believe that he cared just as much for her
welfare as he did their child's. But she doubted she would
ever know. Whatever went on in Liam's heart stayed there.

"Oh, Liam, it isn't necessary for you to go all the way
to El Paso with me. With Clayton gone, I'll need you here
more than ever. The trip will only be for one night and
when I get back I'll tell you everything the doctor said.
You do trust me to tell you everything, don't you?"

"Sure. I just thought—well, when Felicia was pregnant
I didn't accompany her. She was independent that way and
practical. You're different from her. Very different. And I
thought you might like the company. That's all."

Was he trying to tell her that he'd missed the opportunity to be a part of Felicia's pregnancy, but that he wanted
things with Kitty to be different? The idea was bittersweet

and for a moment she closed her eyes and wondered how or why she'd ever fallen for a widower. It would have been so much simpler if she'd fallen in love with a man who wasn't carrying a ghost around with him.

Holding back a sigh, she glanced at him. "I would like the company," she said softly. "But the timing is bad. Why don't we plan for both of us to go next time? I think the doctor might do another ultrasound then."

A faint smile touched one corner of his lips. "It's a date."

The next morning Kitty had to be at the airport before seven. Liam insisted on driving her and she didn't argue the point. She was already dreading the time she'd be away from him, but she was determined not to make an issue of parting. He'd said that his first wife had been independent and practical, so it only made sense that those were the traits he admired in a woman.

Kitty could be independent when need be. God knows, she'd had to learn how to stand on her own two feet since her father had died. But practicality was another matter. To Kitty, everything in life wasn't supposed to make common sense or be matter-of-fact. Dreams of the future were as much a part of her as the dirt she got under her fingernails whenever she cleaned out a nasty hoof. And those dreams included romance and a man that whispered love and devotion in her ear. She needed those things as much or more than her ranch and the horses that went with it. Yet as she peered into the future, she wasn't sure she would have any of those things in her life.

When they arrived at the airport, the traffic was hectic. Liam finally managed to maneuver the truck through a maze of cars and taxis until he found an open spot near the curbed sidewalk leading into the terminal.

While he parked, Kitty gripped the small tote carrying the few personal items she'd need overnight and waited for him to come around to her side of the truck to help her to the ground.

Once the two of them were standing on the sidewalk, she found herself leaning against him and hating to release the grip she had on his arm.

"Have you arranged for anyone to pick you up in El Paso?" he asked.

"Yes. Natalie, my racing manager, will be there."

A gust of wind swept through the covered access and whipped a strand of Kitty's hair across her face. He quickly reached for it and her heart ached with longing as he gently tucked it behind her ear.

If only he would pull her into his arms and tell her that he loved her and would be counting the minutes until she returned, Kitty thought. But love wasn't on Liam's mind or in his plans. She had to make do with the physical affection he gave her.

"Do you have your cell and everything else you need? Money, credit cards?"

Her throat tightened. "Yes. I'll be fine, Liam."

His hand rested protectively on the upper part of her stomach. "You will call as soon as you've seen the doctor?"

He did care. Very much. So why wasn't that enough to make the ache in her heart go away? Was she selfish to want more than he was willing to give?

"I promise."

His gaze searched hers for long moments and then with a soft groan, he bent his head and pressed a kiss on her lips. For a brief second Kitty's hands clung to his shoulders. But all too soon he eased back and gave her a slow smile.

"You'd better go in. I'm sure the lines are long. And you don't want to miss your flight."

Nodding, she tried to swallow the lump in her throat. "I'll see you tomorrow night," she said.

He nodded in reply, and she turned and hurried toward the entrance. She'd gotten only a few steps away when she heard him call out her name and she whirled around, her heart pounding with hopeful anticipation.

But instead of finding herself suddenly wrapped in his arms, he was still standing several feet away, his hand lifted in a simple farewell. "Goodbye, Kitty."

She blinked at the tears burning her eyes. "Goodbye," she called out to him, then hurried into the terminal before she broke into sobs.

Chapter Nine

That night when Liam left barn 59 he didn't drive straight home. The thought of going home and not finding Kitty there was not at all inviting so he stopped by a local watering hole that racetrack personnel frequented.

He was sitting at the bar, staring into a mug of dark beer when he felt a hand come down on his shoulder. Glancing around, he saw Andy straddling the stool next to him.

"It's hell when a guy can't even go to a bar and get away from his boss," the young groom jokingly greeted. "What are you doing here, anyway? I didn't even know you drank beer."

Liam grunted with faint amusement. "There's a lot you don't know about me."

"That's the damned truth," Andy muttered. "None of us knew you ever looked at a woman and then suddenly you're married and going to have a baby. The CIA is more open than you are."

The barmaid, a young brunette with a wide smile and dark eyes, ambled over to Andy to take his order. After she left to fetch his beer, Liam said, "A person learns more when he listens."

"Yeah. If you have someone to listen to," Andy replied then slanted a questioning glance at Liam. "So why aren't you home with your new wife?"

"She had to fly to Texas."

"Oh. So she leaves and you're out drinking. That doesn't look good."

Liam grimaced. "You're supposed to be watching ten horses. Instead, you're here drinking. That doesn't look good, either," he retorted.

Andy shrugged and Liam noticed the kid wasn't even bothered enough to look embarrassed. A fact that hardly surprised him. Andy was an independent sprout who'd always spoken candidly. And even though he sometimes irritated the hell out of Liam, he'd come to respect the groom's self-confidence.

"Don't worry. I didn't shove my share of the work onto Clint. The girls offered to watch the horses while I came over here for a beer. I promised them I wouldn't be gone long."

Liam shook his head. "Andy, you could charm a frog into jumping off a lily pad."

The barmaid shoved a beer in front of Andy and he chuckled as he lifted the mug up to his face. "I didn't charm, I bribed. Movie tickets for both of them. So why didn't you go with Kitty? Me and Clint could have taken care of things for a few days."

If Liam had thought that Andy was simply being nosy he would have told him to mind his own business. But he understood that this was Andy's way of trying to be helpful.

"She's only going to be gone for one night. And Clayton, her assistant, had a family emergency and had to leave yesterday. I needed to be here to watch over things for her." Plus, she'd not seemed that keen on having her husband join her, Liam thought, as he wrapped his fingers around the sweaty beer mug. The notion bothered him far more than it should have.

"Oh. Well, that shouldn't take much effort. She only has ten horses in the barn. But they are damned good ones," Andy added.

Liam took several swallows of his beer then set the mug aside. "What do you know about her assistant? Anything?"

Andy shot him a quizzical look. "Clayton is your wife's assistant. You ought to know more about him than me."

"He's worked for Desert End for over a year now. That's about all I know," Liam told him. "I just don't question her about her staff. And she doesn't question me about mine."

"I see. Well, I can tell you that half the women working in the barn have a crush on Clayton," Andy said with a grimace.

Liam grunted. "What about the other half?"

Andy chuckled shrewdly. "They have a crush on you."

Not amused, Liam shook his head. "They'll get over it."

Andy reached for a pretzel stick lying in a nearby basket. "Why do you ask? You think he's not good enough?"

Liam wiped a hand over his face. It wasn't like him to speak about such personal things to anyone, even his family. But tonight he felt the need to talk and Andy, with his long hair and tattoos, was an open-minded guy who generally accepted a person no matter how strange or complex the situation.

"Will never hired fools to work at Desert End. And from what I've picked up, Clayton seems to know his business damned well." He also seemed very close to Kitty

and she to him. That bothered Liam. Even if their relationship was platonic, Liam wanted to be the guy that his
wife needed and turned to whenever she had a problem.

Andy remained silent for a few moments as he chugged
down a portion of his beer. At the opposite end of the
room, a tall lanky woman with a braid hanging down her
back kept feeding the jukebox. The slow, mournful bal-
lads did little to help Liam's somber mood. Plus the music
kept reminding him of the night he'd taken Kitty out dining and dancing to celebrate Awesome Joe's win. She'd
felt so warm and natural in his arms, so right. He'd enjoyed that night more than he could remember enjoying
anything. But later, after they'd made love, she'd turned
quiet, almost distant and he'd lain there wondering what
she was thinking, feeling. He'd even wanted to ask her
those things. But he'd been afraid to put the questions into
words. Afraid he might learn he was nothing more than
a bed partner to her, the man who just happened to sow
the seed in her fertile womb.

*Just what do you want, Liam? For Kitty to love you
madly, deeply, like she's never loved any other man?*

No! He didn't want her love! That would make him feel
too caught. Too committed. He didn't want love to be between them. The emotion was fragile and risky, just like
life itself. He didn't want to take the chance of experiencing that much passion again and then having it ripped
away from him.

Andy's voice suddenly interrupted Liam's torn
thoughts. "Right after Mr. Cartwright died I heard that
Desert End was going to be sold. When Kitty showed up
here with the horses I figured the story wasn't true."

Liam looked at him. "Who told you such a thing?"

"I think Clint told me. He heard it from someone out
at Sunland Park when we were there this past winter."

Frowning, Liam said flatly, "Well, whoever said such a thing didn't know what they were talking about. Will wouldn't have left instructions for the ranch to be sold. It and the horses belong to Kitty and she damned sure wouldn't sell."

"Yeah. I suspected it was only gossip. You can hear anything around the track and most of it is a bunch of bull."

Families always behave differently at home than in public.

Kitty's words suddenly drifted through Liam's mind and now he wondered exactly what she'd meant by that. Had Willard Cartwright been a different man than the one he'd presented to the public, to Liam? If so, maybe there was a grain of truth to the gossip Andy and Clint had heard. But no. He couldn't believe that Will would be so mean to sell his daughter's home and livelihood out from under her. It didn't make any sense.

"You're right about that. You can always hear rumors around the barn," Liam said. After throwing a few bills on the countertop to take care of his and Andy's beer, he rose to his feet and slapped a hand against the young man's back. "See you in the morning."

"Yeah. Four-thirty," Andy replied. "And don't let me catch you being late."

Liam chuckled. "Have you ever?"

A wry grin twisted Andy's lean face. "No. But I keep trying."

Later that night, some thirty miles northeast of El Paso, Kitty was sitting in the back courtyard and staring up at the endless sky dotted with stars. She'd always loved this quiet spot where the landscaping made it feel as though she was sitting out in the desert, while being completely surrounded by the secure walls of her home. That's why she'd chosen to have her wedding in this exact spot. But tonight the urge to weep had been lingering just beneath the surface of her emotions and she wasn't exactly sure what was tearing at her the most. Being away from Liam or worrying that Desert End would soon be taken away from her.

"Here you are! I've been looking all through the house for you."

The voice came from behind her and Kitty turned her head to see Natalie, her racing manager and longtime friend striding toward her.

The petite brunette looked significantly younger than her thirty-six years, while her beauty always turned male heads. Kitty had often asked the woman why she'd never married. But Natalie always insisted her job was far more interesting than a man.

"I wanted to sit outside a few minutes before I went to bed," Kitty explained.

Natalie sank into a wicker lawn chair angled to the left of Kitty's. "You didn't eat very much for dinner this evening. Are you feeling okay?"

"I'm okay. Just trying not to overdo it on the calories. I don't want to give the doctor a shock tomorrow morning when he looks at my weight."

Natalie chuckled. "You look just right, honey. Even with the belly."

Resting her head against the back of the chair, Kitty said, "You're not a very good liar, Nattie. Whenever I look in the mirror I see drab skin and tired circles beneath my eyes. But I guess that goes along with being pregnant."

"Being pregnant isn't the problem. It's your job." Shaking her head with disgust, Natalie swiped a hand through her thick black hair. "If I'd had any clue that your father had put such a ridiculous stipulation in his will I would have contested his sanity. Really!"

Kitty sighed. Other than her brother, Natalie was the only person who knew about the conditions that Willard had made clear in his will. She'd not wanted to explain any of it to Clayton or Bella. She didn't want any of the Desert End employees worrying about their job security if she could possibly avoid it. And God willing, they'd never have to hear about this enormous test that her father had put upon her shoulders.

"You sound like Owen now. Please don't tell me you're starting to think I need to get out of the business."

"Not in the least," Natalie replied then blew out a frustrated breath. "I'm angry that Will has done this to you."

"Well, to be fair, before Dad died, he didn't have any idea that I was pregnant. Especially with Liam's child. If he had—well, I just don't think he would've put such a test on me."

"Is that what you're calling it? A test?"

"What else?" Kitty countered. "Maybe he wanted me to be sure that training was the vocation I really wanted for the rest of my life? And let's face it, he'd poured his sweat into building this place, his reputation on the track. He didn't want me screwing it all up."

"Or maybe he wanted to still have control over you even after he was gone," Natalie said with undisguised sarcasm. "Kitty, the man was wonderful in so many ways. Yet he could be so infuriating. By all rights you should hate him for what he's doing to you."

A wan smile crossed Kitty's face. "I can't. In spite of his faults I loved him."

Natalie's sigh was tinged with regret. "Yes. So did I."

"It's too late to change anything now. I simply have to do my best and pray it's enough."

Natalie snorted. "Your best! Damn it all, Will was a good trainer, but even he never won the Hollywood Oaks! Why would he expect you to do more? It was mean and barbaric of him to do such a thing to his daughter!"

"Well, if you're worried about your job, don't be. You're an excellent racing manager. There're plenty of trainers who'd love to hire you."

"Maybe so. But Desert End is my home. I don't want to uproot any more than you do."

Uproot? Kitty couldn't think about roots, period. The lifelong ties she had to Desert End were so fragile at the moment they were barely hanging together. And even if they did, she was married now. She didn't know where Liam wanted to set down roots or if he ever would. He didn't talk to her about long-term issues. His conversations about the future always seemed to stop once the baby was born.

"Well, who knows, if Owen does wind up with the place he might sell it to another horse breeder or trainer and you wouldn't have to leave."

Her features tight, Natalie scooted to the edge of her chair. "As far as I'm concerned, Owen is a bastard—that's all I have to say about him. And don't worry about me for one second, Kitty. This isn't about me. It's about you and this ranch." She waved a hand around her head. "Sure, it's beautiful and I love living here, working here. But it's not worth you killing yourself over or putting the baby's health in danger. Just remember that."

"I'm not about to do that, Natalie. If things get too much for me to handle, Clayton will pick up the load."

"Sure. If he's around. What are you going to do if he has to stay away for an extended length of time?"

"He won't," Kitty said with more confidence than she

was feeling. "He'll be back as soon as his father is out of danger. In the meantime, Liam will help."

From the corner of her eye, Natalie studied her keenly. "You still haven't told Liam about the will?"

Bending her head, Kitty sighed. "I can't."

"Why not?" Natalie demanded. "He needs to know. You're his wife!"

"Desert End has nothing to do with him. Besides, it's too complicated. With the baby and everything. I have a feeling— No, I'm quite certain he's going to be upset."

Natalie's short laugh was incredulous. "Who wouldn't be upset?"

"I'm not talking about my father's edict. Well, it's a cinch Liam would be shocked about it. But he's going to…I'm afraid he's going to misconstrue the whole reason I married him. He's going to think I'd planned on using him as a trainer to make sure Black Dahlia saves the day."

"Bah!" Natalie waved a dismissive hand through the air. "You can fix that problem easily enough. You can tell him the truth—why you really married him."

Kitty stared in disbelief at the other woman. "I can't! He doesn't want to hear that I love him. Love doesn't have anything to do with our relationship—our marriage."

"It does where you're concerned."

Like the grip of a hand, pain squeezed Kitty's heart. "Yes. But that doesn't matter. We've not been married that long. I don't want to stir things up. Especially before the baby gets here."

Natalie released a disgusted groan. "Let's see if I have all of this straight. You don't want to tell him about your father's will because he'll be upset. And you don't want him to know you love him because that would displease him. What can you talk to the man about? How did you two ever make a baby together?"

Kitty's cheeks burned. "Making a baby doesn't require talking."

"So it doesn't," Natalie shot back at her. "But I think you'd better start doing a lot of it and fast. Or this whole thing is going to blow up in your face. The race is coming. The baby is coming. He needs to understand just how much your home means to you. How much *he* means to you."

Lifting her head, Kitty looked at her friend. "Look, Natalie, the man still loves the wife he lost, the wife he chose to have in his life. Because of the baby I was thrust upon him. He'll never see me in the same way he saw her."

"I wouldn't want him to. He needs to see you as the wonderful woman that you are. Not as a substitute for a ghost."

Pressing her fingertips against her forehead, Kitty slowly shook her head. "Natalie, I appreciate your concern. But you've never been married."

"And seeing the misery you're in, I'm not sure I'd ever want to be."

Kitty didn't make any sort of reply to that and after a moment, Natalie said, "All this worrying can't be good for you. I'm concerned about you, Kitty. Between the physical work and the mental torture you're going through I..."

A footstep sounded behind them and the remainder of Natalie's words trailed away as both women looked around to see Kitty's brother striding toward them. In jeans, khaki uniform shirt and a tan Stetson he looked every inch a Texas lawman and just as formidable. Kitty could only wonder what he was doing here on the ranch since he rarely showed his face on the property, even when she and Willard had been at home.

"Good evening, ladies. Care if I join you?"

Her lips a tight line, Natalie quickly rose to her feet.

"Sorry, but you'll have to excuse me. I'm suddenly feeling queasy."

Kitty watched as her brother shot a sly grin at the other woman.

"What's the matter? Eat your own cooking tonight?"

Natalie sneered at him. "Why don't you go arrest somebody? That is what you do best, isn't it?"

His chuckle was just arrogant enough to make Kitty look away and Natalie stomp off.

"Oh, I wouldn't say that," he called after the manager. "I'm pretty good at a few other things."

"Was that necessary?" Kitty asked her brother as he eased his lanky frame into the chair Natalie had vacated. "She already thinks you're an ogre. Why do you go out of your way to make matters worse?"

"Because it amuses me to see her get so het up. Especially when she's wrong."

Kitty looked at him curiously. "About you being an ogre?"

He grimaced. "About a lot of things."

Kitty didn't press for an explanation. Whatever the rift was between him and Natalie was their business. She had plenty of her own problems to deal with without barrowing more.

"So what brings you out to the ranch tonight?" she asked. "You're not working?"

"I just finished up. Had to transfer a prisoner to El Paso County jail. I heard this morning that you were going to be home. So I thought I'd drop by and see how you're doing."

He sounded sincere enough, but with Owen she could never be quite sure. Even though there were ten years between their ages and their personalities were quite different, they'd always been close as siblings. Even so, Owen was a guy who was hard to read. Oftentimes, he could say one thing and mean another.

"Don't you mean you stopped by to see if I was cracking and about to collapse?"

"Don't be nasty, Kitty. That's my field." He settled back in his chair and crossed his boots at his ankles. "So how is my little niece or nephew doing?"

She patted her growing belly. "I go to the doctor in the morning. But so far, so good."

"If the doctor has any sense, he'll tell you to stay home and away from those damned horses."

"I don't want to hear it, Owen," she said firmly. "Pregnant women do all sorts of physical jobs and do them well with no ill effects. I should be no exception."

"Damn it, Kitty. I'm not trying to be mean or vengeful. I love you."

She blew out a heavy sigh. "Your attitude has nothing to do with the baby or loving me. You never wanted me to follow Dad into the field of horse racing. Now that I'm going to become a mother you think that gives you more cause to berate and dictate to me. Well, listen to this news flash. I intend to do this job for the rest of my life. No matter how short or long that happens to be!"

His nostrils flaring, he shot her a disgusted look. "I suppose now that you have Liam at your beck and call, you think you have the Oaks in the bag. Well, even he loses races, my dear sister."

It was just like Owen to be hateful in the name of love. At times he was so much like their father it amazed her.

Tight-lipped, she wasted no time in correcting him. "Liam isn't training Black Dahlia, I am. And just in case you're interested, she's training at top form right now. So don't start counting this ranch as yours yet."

Lifting his hat, he ran a hand through his thick, dark

hair. When he looked at her again, his features had softened, but his voice hadn't. "Oh, sis, it's not this ranch I'm wanting. I want things to be different for you. But I can see that you're not going to change. You're just like Dad. Dead set on living your life at the track or the barn. I was hoping this baby would change you. But that was before I learned it was Liam's. With him as a father, the poor thing will probably grow up sleeping in a feed tub or worse."

Kitty momentarily closed her eyes and fought to hang on to her patience. "Just what is it that you want from me, Owen? I don't try to tell you what your job should be. Or who you should marry—not that any woman would or could put up with you," she added drily while piercing him with a pointed look. "Why do you have to be so much like Dad? I'm not stupid. I can make my own choices in life without you doing them for me."

"You're making your choices with your heart instead of your head, Kitty. That's foolish."

"How would you know?" she shot back at him. "You've never tried it."

He scowled at her. "If you do lose that race, Kitty, I will see that Dad's wishes are carried out. And if you think my resolve on the matter will weaken, then you're in for a surprise."

Not in the mood to listen to another word, Kitty rose to her feet. "I wouldn't dream of thinking that your heart would ever soften, Owen. But listen to this. I am going to win that race. And you're going to see that I didn't just tag along after Dad in order to travel the country. I did it so that I could become a top trainer. And I'm going to prove my capabilities—not only to you, but to Liam and everyone else. And just so you'll know exactly how much I trust you, someone is guarding Black Dahlia at all times."

Owen's dark eyes narrowed to slits. "Do you honestly think I would harm an animal just to prove my point?"

"Uh, let me think about that for a second." She tapped a finger dumbly against the side of her head. "Yes, I do. Anyone that would threaten to take his sister's home away from her would stop at nothing."

"I'm not trying to take anything away from you," he retorted. "Whether you lose it or not is entirely in your hands."

"Oh, sure. And you're hoping that I fail in the Oaks," she drawled sarcastically. Stepping away from the group of lawn furniture, she started toward the house and her brother followed close on her heels.

"Not exactly," he replied. "But if I thought for a minute that it would make you open your eyes and become a real wife and mother, then yes, I'm hoping you fail."

Whirling on him, she gasped with outrage. "A real wife and mother! You make me sick, Owen. Really sick!"

She jerked open the door and stepped inside a large kitchen. Since Coral and the rest of the house staff had already retired for the evening, the room was empty and Kitty was thankful. She didn't want any Desert End employees hearing cross words being exchanged between the Cartwright siblings. Especially when the argument could affect their jobs.

The two of them paused near the end of a long breakfast bar as Owen continued speaking his mind. "Think about it, Kitty. My mother died. Yours left and cut all ties. And Dad—well, he was always off chasing his dream of getting that next big win. I guess what I'm getting at is that I've always needed you in my life. We've needed each other."

"Of course we do," she agreed.

He rolled his eyes with disbelief. "That's hard for me

to believe. You're off chasing Dad's dream. And I'm self-ish enough to want you around. I don't want the child you're carrying to grow up without a mother like the two of us have."

Other than an aunt who lived some hundred miles away from Desert End, Kitty and Owen had no close relatives. But now Kitty had Liam and the coming baby. And for the present, she was living in California. Maybe Owen was feeling excluded and selfishly wanting his sister to remain home on the ranch. But it wasn't her responsibility to keep her brother happy.

"Owen, believe me, I will be a full-time mother. Besides, how I mother my own child is my decision. Not yours. And now that we're on the subject, you could have a family of your own. But you've chosen not to. That's not my fault."

He looked away from her, but for one split second before he turned his face aside, she'd thought she'd spotted pained shadows in his eyes. Could it be that her brother wasn't nearly as tough as he wanted everyone to believe? Oh, God, she wanted him to be happy, but not at her own expense.

"No," he muttered. "I don't expect it's anyone's fault but my own."

Before she could make any sort of reply, he bent his head and placed a kiss on her forehead. "I gotta go. I hope your doctor's visit goes well tomorrow."

She kissed his cheek and for a brief moment, hugged him close. "If anything is amiss, I'll let you know," she promised. "Take care of yourself."

"I will."

He left the room and after a moment she heard the door at the front of the house open and close. The hollow sound filled her with sadness.

* * *

The next morning, Kitty's visit to the medical clinic went quite well, with everything checking out perfectly. Before she left the building, she immediately called Liam with the news and the sound of his happy voice made her even more eager to get back to California and his side.

By late that evening, her flight touched down at LAX and she spotted Liam waiting for her inside the terminal. He was holding a bouquet of white tulips and purple hyacinth and the smile on his face was like a light to the dark clouds in her heart.

Her steps quickened, speeding her across the concourse, until she reached him and then she flung herself at him as though they'd been apart for weeks rather than a day.

"Oh, Liam, it's so nice to be back!" Gripping him tightly, she kissed both sides of his face and then his mouth.

The hunger she tasted in his kiss warmed her blood and by the time the contact of their lips ended, she was practically breathless.

"I hope you like tulips," he said as he eased back far enough to offer her the bouquet. Kitty bent to the fragrant blooms of hyacinth and she took a moment to draw in their lovely scent before situating them carefully in the corner of one arm.

"I never expected flowers. Is there a special occasion I don't know about?" she asked as she used her free arm to latch around his.

"They're just to let you know how much I missed you," he said softly.

He'd gotten the flowers for her! Just for her! Not for the baby. Not for winning a race. Not for any other reason, but her! The simple gesture filled her with happiness.

"I've missed you, too, Liam," she whispered huskily. "Very much."

Their gazes met and her heart thudded at the smoldering promises she saw in his hazel-green eyes.

"Come on," he said lowly. "Let's get home."

Home. Kitty wasn't sure where her home was anymore. But as she walked alongside Liam, her arm clinging tightly to his, she wanted to believe that wherever her husband was that's where her home would be.

But he didn't love her, she thought dismally. And a home could never survive without love to keep its foundation solid.

Kitty had sworn to fight to hold on to Desert End, but it suddenly dawned on her that winning the Oaks and securing the ranch wasn't the only monumental task she had facing her. She had to win Liam's heart. Without it, she could never be happy or whole.

Chapter Ten

Later that night as the two of them lay in bed, Kitty rested on her side, her cheek cradled against the pillow as she gazed drowsily at the silvery moonlight streaming beneath the draped curtain.

She wanted to believe that what had just transpired between her and Liam had been making love. At least, to her it had been giving her body to him with all her heart and soul. But in spite of the hunger he'd displayed, the eagerness and gentleness he'd shown her, she had no idea what the driving force was behind his kisses and caresses. Even now, as his fingertips made a leisurely trail up and down her spine she had no idea what he was really thinking and feeling.

He needs to know exactly why you married him.

Ever since Kitty had rushed into Liam's arms at the airport, Natalie's words had been haunting her, and she realized the other woman was right. Even if Liam didn't love her, he needed to know the depth of her feelings for him.

"Without you here last night, this bed was like sleeping on the cold ground," he admitted, his voice low and husky. "I almost stayed at the barn and slept in my office instead."

Her heart thumped as she tried to summon the courage she needed. "Awesome Joe might have let you sleep with him. He would have kept you warm," she gently teased.

"Hmm." He nuzzled his lips against the side of her neck. "Joe kicks and you don't."

The smell of him, the feel of his hands on her skin, the deep masculine sound of his voice never ceased to thrill her and she realized that no man before Liam had ever made her feel so alive, so much a woman. But that wasn't why she was having his baby. Or why she'd married him.

Catching his hand with hers, she brought his fingers to her lips and kissed each callused tip. "I love you, Liam."

Slowly, his head lifted away from hers and even though she couldn't see his face, she could feel his gaze sweeping over her, surveying her as though he'd suddenly found himself in bed with a stranger.

After a few silent moments stretched between them, she rolled onto her back to see him staring solemnly down at her.

"Have I shocked you?" she asked softly. "I thought you'd probably already guessed how I feel. Either way, I felt you needed to know."

"Why?"

Her heart sank at his clipped, one-word response. "Aren't husbands and wives supposed to tell each other these things?" she asked.

Sighing, he looked away from her. "Yes. But—"

"But what?"

"We're not—" His troubled gaze swung back to her face. "Things are different with us."

Clutching the sheet to her bare breasts, she scooted to a sitting position. "You mean we're not the typical married couple."

"Not exactly."

"Hmm. Funny that you should say that, Liam. Your argument for us to marry was to make a 'real' family for our child."

A groan of frustration sounded in his throat. "That's true. But I didn't say anything about love. Love has nothing to do with us—or our marriage."

Pain was crushing the middle of her chest, but she did her best not to let it show. Not for anything did she want him to see the power he wielded over her.

She said, "That's not the way I see it."

He grimaced then lifted his gaze toward the dark ceiling. "I never asked you to love me."

Her throat so tight she could barely speak, she said, "That's true. You didn't. And I'll never ask you to love me. I'd be wasting my time anyway."

That jerked his attention back on her face and he stared at her, his expression a mixture of anguish, confusion and curiosity.

"What does that mean?"

She slid off the bed and reached for the satin robe that had fallen to the floor when Liam had pushed it off her shoulders.

As she tied the sash above the mound of their baby, she answered, "Just what I said. I'd be wasting my time. You can't love me or any woman, for that matter. You're too busy hanging on to your dead wife."

He sucked in a harsh breath. "That's an awful thing to say."

She paused to look over her shoulder, and her heart winced at the raw pain she saw on his face.

"The truth can be awful," she said, then with a sigh of regret she turned back to him. "Liam, I'm not trying to censure you. I'm just stating a fact. I married you knowing how you feel. And I'm not trying to change you now. I simply wanted you to know that I love you. How you feel about me in return is your business."

Like a man who'd suddenly been shot at and needed to scramble to safety, he vaulted off the bed and wrapped his hands around her shoulders.

"Damn it, Kitty, why did you have to do this? To ruin everything? It's all been going so well. We get along—we respect each other. We don't need love coming between us—interfering and messing up all that's good."

So her love was a problem he could do without, she thought sickly. God, what a fool she'd been for ever listening to Natalie's advice! But more than that, she'd been an even bigger fool to allow her heart to hope and dream and love this man.

"Don't worry, Liam," she said stiffly, her back proud and straight. "You won't hear the word from me again."

She pulled away from him and started toward a door that led into the bathroom, but he caught up to her before she reached it.

"Kit, you don't understand," he said in a torn voice. "I do have feelings for you, but…"

His words trailed off as she fixed her gaze on his. She felt drained and empty inside and she supposed he could see that dullness in her eyes. "Look, Liam, if you feel like I've put you on a hook or something, then forget it. I don't expect anything from you. Except that you be a good father to our child. The rest is just inconsequential."

"Kitty—"

"I'm going to take a shower and get some sleep," she told him. "I need to get to the track very early in the morning. With Clayton still gone I have lots to do."

Before he could say anything else, she slipped into the bathroom and shut the door behind her. But once the sound of the shower could drown out the sounds of her sobs, she sat down on the tiled floor and with her hands covering her face, wept until there were no more tears inside her.

From that night on, Kitty's relationship with Liam changed drastically and as the weekend came and passed, she continued to ask herself if Liam might have spoken the truth when he'd said her vow of love would ruin everything between them. Because it appeared that it had.

Not that either was angry or resentful or throwing nasty accusations at each other. In fact, they never spoke crossly to each other. But then they rarely had time to talk, period. With the racing meet going full force, they were both caught up in their daily schedules. Nevertheless, when the two of them were alone, the easy companionship they'd always shared before was gone, only to be replaced by awkward tension.

To her utter relief, the following Sunday saw Black Dahlia win a Grade II race by a full half-length over her nearest competitor. Kitty hadn't wasted any time in texting Owen to let him know that the filly was moving forward and promising to be a champion. He'd written a one word reply. *Congratulations*.

That one word would have meant a lot to Kitty if her brother had sent it with sincerity. But he'd made it clear how he felt about the business and how she should be living her life. She couldn't change his way of thinking, so all she could do was prove him wrong. As for her marriage, she didn't know where it was headed or how it could ever possibly change. She only knew that with the baby coming this should be one of the happiest times in her life. Instead, she'd never been more miserable.

A week and a half after Dahlia's spectacular performance, the weather turned cool and damp, especially for a late-May morning in California. Bundled in a heavy denim ranch jacket with a bright yellow scarf tied around her neck, she was making her way down the shed row when she heard a male voice call to her from behind.

Pausing in her tracks, she glanced over her shoulder and was completely surprised to see Clayton striding toward her. The sight of her dedicated assistant was such a relief, she cried out with joy and hurried to meet him.

"Clayton! You didn't let me know you were returning!" she scolded, then stepping forward, gave him a huge hug.

He laughed as he glanced down at the mound of baby separating them. "Wow! You've grown since I've been gone."

Pulling a playful face at him, Kitty said, "You've only been gone for two weeks or so. I couldn't look that much bigger. But I am getting toward my eighth month of pregnancy and that's when the baby starts putting on weight. I guess it's starting to show." She stepped back from him. "So how's your father? I got your note saying he'd had surgery and was improving."

"He's going to be released from the hospital tomorrow. And my sister will be there with my mother to help her get him settled. His recovery will take some time but the doctors expect him to be able to live a normal life— if he takes care of himself and follows orders. He's one of the lucky ones."

Clayton looked almost guilty, as though it wasn't right that his father had survived a heart incident while Kitty's had died. But now, more than ever, she understood that things happened for a reason and sometimes there was nothing fair about them.

"Very," Kitty agreed then kindly patted his arm. "I'm so glad you're back. I guess you've been keeping up with racing results—Dahlia won her race by a half-length. Now it's on to the Oaks."

"How did she come out of it?"

"Even better than I expected. Her appetite is great. She's sound and happy. No glitches at all." For the first time in days, Kitty felt good enough to smile. Liam might not give a damn about her or her stable of horses, but at least Clayton did. "I'm actually beginning to believe we have a legitimate shot at this, Clayton."

"I never doubted you, or her, for one minute."

If only Liam would say those words to her, she thought. Instead, he was slowly but surely starting to throw out comments about her long work hours and the stress she was putting on her body. Each time he brought up the subject, Kitty wanted to scream that he was the one putting the most stress on her. Not her job.

Snagging a hold on his jacket sleeve, she urged him forward. "Let's go have a look at her," Kitty suggested. "I want to see what you think."

The two of them had traveled only a few steps when Liam suddenly appeared from a nearby tack room. As they paused to greet him, Liam's flinty gaze swept over Kitty, then settled on Clayton.

"Clayton's father is doing well now," Kitty told him. "So he's back to work. Isn't it great?"

"Yeah. Great," Liam answered with sarcasm, then turned his attention to Clayton. "Maybe you can get my wife to ease up and let you take care of things now. She doesn't seem to want to listen to me."

Before Kitty or Clayton could make any sort of reply,

Liam strode off without another word. Swamped with disappointment and embarrassment, she pressed the back of her hand against her lips and shook her head.

"I'm sorry, Clayton—I apologize for my husband's curtness," she told her assistant. "He's not been himself here lately." Not since he learned that his wife was in love with him, she thought bitterly. She didn't understand why her revelation had disturbed him so, or why he was seemingly trying to distance himself from her now. She only knew that his attitude was killing her and she was swiftly reaching the breaking point.

The other man looked at her with concern. "What's happened? Don't bother trying to answer that," he quickly added. "I tried to tell you that Liam Donovan was a bastard. So now that you've signed the wedding certificate, he's starting to show his true colors."

"Oh, God, Clayton, don't start," she pleaded. "He isn't a bad man. He just has some issues he's dealing with right now."

"The only thing on your husband's agenda right now should be you and your well-being," he said hotly. "Nothing else! And I'm just the man that can remind him of that!"

"Don't you dare!" Kitty warned. "Your business is seeing after the horses. I'll deal with my husband."

That night Liam was already home when Kitty got there. She tossed her handbag onto the cabinet counter and sank into a chair at the table where he was already eating something he'd grabbed at the deli.

"Is there more where that came from?" Kitty asked.

He jerked a thumb toward the refrigerator. "Since you were so late showing up I put it in there."

Rising to her feet, Kitty moved over to the cabinet and

rinsed her hands at the sink. "I had an owner show up at the track. I couldn't leave," she explained. "Not after he'd traveled all the way from Santa Fe to check on his horse."

"Clayton couldn't have dealt with the man? What do you pay him for? Just to strut around the barn?"

His comment was so off-the-wall that Kitty didn't even make an effort to reply. She walked over to the refrigerator and pulled the foam containers of food from the shelf. "I'm sorry my work has kept me so busy here lately, Liam. But so has yours."

"I'm not the one who's pregnant," he said tersely.

She turned away from the cabinet to glare at him. "I'm so glad you realize that," she drawled sarcastically.

Tossing down his napkin, he left the table and walked over to her. The tenseness on his face was gone and a part of her melted as his hand came up to cradle her cheek.

"I'm sorry, Kitty. I don't want to sound like a—"

"Bastard? That's what Clayton calls you."

He grimaced. "No doubt. The man doesn't like me for many reasons. The main one being you."

"He wants me to be happy—for us to be happy."

His hands slipped to her shoulders and began to knead the taut flesh. "I'm trying, Kitty, but it's hard to be happy when I'm constantly worrying about you. Felicia was about seven months or so when she—" He broke off, then shook his head. "Well, ever since you made that trip last month to El Paso you've been different with me. And driven with your work. I can see how tired you're getting. This thing with Dahlia is getting out of hand. You eat, sleep and breathe that filly. It's not healthy for you or the baby!"

She silently groaned. "You, more than anyone, ought to understand how important the Oaks are to me. Dahlia's victory would solidify my barn's success."

"Your barn is already considered successful. You don't have to prove anything."

Oh, God, if only he knew, she thought. And maybe now was her opportunity to tell him about her father's will. Natalie believed that Liam should know about the conditions Willard had placed on her, but Kitty wasn't convinced it would help anything. She'd made a mistake when she'd taken Natalie's advice and told Liam that she loved him. Telling him about the will might be an even bigger mistake.

"That's not true. Dad isn't running things and calling the shots anymore. It's me. I do have to prove myself."

"Not at the expense of my baby."

My baby. My baby.

The words pierced her heart. With Liam everything came down to the baby. It was the only reason he'd married her and the only reason he was likely to stay married to her. That day she'd returned from El Paso and he'd given her the flowers, she'd let herself believe that he was changing, that he was beginning to consider her just as important to him as the baby. That's why she'd let those words of love slip out of her that night. She'd been wrong. And she couldn't let herself make that mistake again.

"Liam, I'm not endangering the baby. If I thought I was—"

"Kitty, I'm asking you to let up," he said gently. "At least leave the house later in the mornings and get home earlier in the evenings."

He wasn't making demands; he was asking and because he was, she felt she had to make concessions for him and their marriage. For years she'd been fighting against her father and her brother to hold on to her own identity and she intended to keep on fighting for it. But she also wanted to make her husband happy.

"I promise that I'll shorten my hours and that I'll rest as much as possible. And as soon as the Oaks is over—"

"The Oaks! The baby is due that very day!"

When Kitty had learned that the baby was due on or about the same day that the American Oaks had been scheduled to run, she'd wondered if it was a cruel twist of fate or a blessed sign from heaven. And she supposed she wouldn't know until it was all over.

Casting him an imploring smile, she said, "And you may have to take over for me during that time. You will, won't you?"

Even though there was a wry twist to his lips, the softness in his eyes was something she'd not seen in days and the sight couldn't help but lift her dark spirits.

"Clayton is back," he reminded her.

She swung her head back and forth. "He's not you," she said simply.

He let out a helpless groan. "Oh, Kit, you make me so aggravated and miserable at times, but I can't help but want you."

Wrapping her arms around his neck, she rested her forehead against his. "Then maybe you should take me to bed," she suggested, her voice husky with need.

"You've not eaten yet," he whispered.

"You can bring me supper in bed. Later," she added slyly.

"It'll be my pleasure."

He placed a swift kiss on her lips, then lifting her into his arms, carried her straight to their bedroom.

Hours later, Liam sat at a small desk in their bedroom with his laptop computer open in front of him. For the past thirty minutes he'd been trying to work, to concentrate on the data sheets of his horses' recent workouts, but his brain refused to focus on the numbers representing the time fractions and distances. Instead, he kept looking away from the computer, his gaze drawn to the image of Kitty sleeping soundly in their bed.

Something had happened to him that night she'd revealed that she loved him. And though days had since passed, he still didn't quite understand his reaction to her admission. He'd been dazed and humbled, but more than anything he'd been terrified and that fear he'd desperately tried to hide behind a wall of anger and frustration.

Tonight was the first night they'd had sex since she'd spoken that vow of love and the reconnection to his wife had shaken him deeply. Just as he'd known it would. That's why he'd fought so hard to keep his distance, he supposed. To keep his body from wanting; his heart from needing.

But when she touched him tonight in the kitchen, he'd been unable to refuse her or the hungry need that had clawed inside of him for the past two and a half weeks. He'd made love to her and now he was beginning to wonder if he was falling in love with her. If he was doing the very thing he'd sworn never to do again.

Kitty loves you. And she wants you to love her back. She needs for you to love her back. And you've fallen short. You make love to her, but you refuse to give her your love. That's not enough to make her happy, Liam. Or to keep her by your side.

Stifling a groan, Liam clicked a button to shut down the computer. He couldn't work with thoughts of Kitty consuming his mind. And he sure as hell couldn't concentrate with that dratted *L* word rattling around and around in his overworked brain.

A big part of being a man was being able to give his woman what she needed and wanted. For the past two weeks Liam had gone around feeling like a complete bastard for being such a failure. No one had to tell him that Kitty was unhappy. Even though she tried to disguise her feelings, he could see the sadness in her eyes, hear it in her voice and that alone was enough to make him miserable.

Now Liam was feeling like a bear being cornered by a determined hunter and the only way he could escape was to fight his way out. But after tonight he was afraid he was losing the fight.

Clicking off the light, he climbed back into bed and turned his face into the long blond hair spilling over his wife's shoulder. Sex wasn't just sex anymore, he thought. And this ache in his heart felt dangerously close to love.

Chapter Eleven

For the next three weeks Kitty's girth grew much heavier, causing her steps to slow and her energy to dwindle. She tried to hide her fatigue, but she wasn't fooling Liam. However, in keeping with her promise she had shortened her working hours at the track and she was allowing him and Clayton to take over more of the tasks that she usually handled herself. But as far as Liam was concerned she needed total rest at home with her feet up and a maid to wait on her.

But Kitty wasn't the let-someone-else-do-it-for-her type and Liam was slowly beginning to see that he'd be putting her under worse stress if he tried to order her to stay home and away from the horses.

This evening, Liam was determined to drive her home at an earlier hour and after finding her office empty, he'd gone through her end of the barn, searching for her in every stall. He was nearing Black Dahlia's stall when he heard her voice and what she was saying caused him to pause before he reached the half gate. Standing partially hidden by the stuffed hay bag swinging at the side of the stall door, he listened as Clayton made a remark about the filly's feeding schedule.

"Clayton, I want you and you alone to inspect Dahlia's feed before it's given to her. And whatever you do, make sure that someone is in or near this stall at all times. I do not want her left alone. Not for any reason."

Liam frowned to himself. It was clear, not only to him, but to everybody around the track, that Kitty was practically obsessed with her star filly. But this was taking things completely over the top and he couldn't understand it. Kitty wasn't a paranoid person. But the Oaks was one of Hollywood's most prestigious races and there was a huge purse involved. Maybe she simply wanted to be extra careful.

Clayton replied, "Hell, Kitty, we have guards here on the grounds. No one can get in the barn without the proper identification. You make it sound like if we turn our backs, someone might do something sinister to the filly."

"Stranger things have happened. And there might be someone around who'd like to see her lose the race," she muttered, then added, "and don't argue. Just do what I say."

"All right. All right. So when will you be back from El Paso?"

"Tomorrow evening. If everything goes okay with my doctor's checkup there won't be any point in staying longer."

"Liam might want you to stay over another night so that you can rest. Especially since he's going with you."

Liam made himself known by stepping into the stall

and shutting the gate behind him. Both Kitty and her assistant turned to look at him.

"I do want her to rest," he told the other man, "but she's already purchased the round-trip tickets."

"Well, I've been trying to assure your wife that Dahlia and the rest of the herd will be perfectly fine while the two of you are away. If I can't take care of them for twenty-four hours on my own, then I need to be making sandwiches at the local deli or something. I sure as hell don't need to be a racehorse trainer."

Kitty rolled her eyes and let out a weary chuckle. "Okay, Clayton. Give me a break. I'm a pregnant mother hen. I have a right to be overly protective." She walked over to Liam and slipped an arm around the back of his waist. "What do you think of my prodigy?"

Liam smiled drily. "You mean your assistant or the filly?"

Clayton let out a good-natured groan and Kitty laughed. After she'd made it clear to Liam that her assistant considered him a bastard, Liam had set out to change the other man's low opinion of him. These past few weeks he'd been helping Clayton as much as he could, so that the two men could alleviate some of Kitty's workload. The time they'd spent together was allowing the two men to get to know each other better and in the process they were actually becoming friends.

"They both look like they can handle themselves without you around for the next day or two."

Kitty walked over to the filly and kissed her nose. "I'll see you soon, my pretty girl." She looked pointedly at Clayton. "And no treats. No carrots, no fruit or anything unless you give it to her yourself. Understand? And only if she cleans up her oats. Make sure Maryann and Greta have my orders, too."

Clayton assured her of everything one more time, before Liam was finally able to urge her out of the stall and down the shed row.

"Aren't you going a bit overboard with Dahlia?" he asked. "I overheard you telling Clayton to keep someone posted at her stall at all times. I'm beginning to worry that you're getting paranoid, Kitty."

She looked at him sharply, then after a moment shook her head and chuckled. "I guess it appears that way, doesn't it? Like I told Clayton, I'm just a pregnant mother hen. Please humor me on this, Liam. I—I'm just so proud of her and anxious for her to do well. I don't want anything to go wrong."

"Yes. I feel the same way about her," he reasoned. "But to worry that someone might try to sabotage her—that kind of thinking is far left field."

She frowned at him. "Really? Well, tell that to the people in Texas who found their champion dead in his stall after being injected with a toxic cocktail of drugs. I realize that incident occurred several years ago. But it's a terrifying thought."

His features full of concern, he glanced down at her. "Kitty, who would ever want to do such a thing to you?"

She smiled at him, but it was a weak expression. "I hope to heaven not anyone."

The next morning Kitty and Liam's flight arrived in El Paso with just enough time to make her appointment with the doctor. They were both relieved to hear that she and the baby were flourishing, but she was caught off guard when the physician ordered her to quit flying until the baby was born.

"But, Dr. Talman, I have to fly back and forth!" she exclaimed. "I wanted to be here for the birth!"

The older man with a round, gentle face gently patted her shoulder. "The only way you can do that is to stay here in El Paso until you deliver. And given the circumstances of your job, I don't think you want to do that," he reasoned.

Frowning, she looked helplessly to Liam, who'd accompanied her to the examining room, then up to the doctor. "No. I can't. I have responsibilities in California."

"Well, from my best calculations, the baby will be coming sometime during the next three weeks. You don't want to give birth in an airplane," the physician pointed out. "That's why I've contacted an excellent doctor in your area and he's agreed to take you on as his patient throughout the last few weeks of your pregnancy. You'll be seeing him weekly from now until you have the baby. Any problems that come up between now and then, he'll take care of. But of course, I'm always available if you want to call with any question or concern." He scribbled something on the top paper of Kitty's file then slipped his pen into the pocket of his white lab coat. "Now, before I go, do you want to know the sex of the baby, Mr. Donovan? I've offered the information to Kitty during some of her earlier visits, but she insists she wants to be surprised. If you can keep a secret, I can whisper it in your ear."

Liam smiled broadly. "No thanks, Doctor. I like surprises, too."

"Fine," the doctor said, then after shaking hands and wishing the couple good luck, he left the room.

Dazed from this unexpected change in plans, Kitty slowly pulled her shirt back over her belly and began to fumble with the buttons. All along, she'd planned on returning to Desert End during the last week of her pregnancy and having the baby here. It was her home! But she had to be reasonable, and if her delivery time did arrive when the Oaks was due to run, she wanted to be in California. Oh, what a mess she was in!

"I can tell you right now this wasn't the way I'd planned for things to go," she muttered.

"Well, if it's any comfort, things rarely go as we plan them. And babies tend to come whenever they get the urge, not when we want them to."

Lifting her head, she looked at him with anguish. "Liam, I don't want to change doctors at this late date. I don't want to have the baby in California. This is a Texas baby. He or she should be Texas born!"

Smiling gently, he left his seat and once he was at her side, folded his arm around her shoulder and kissed her cheek. "Kit, think of it this way. The baby was conceived in Texas, so it's Texas bred. Nothing can change that."

He was being sweet and understanding and that was enough to take away some of her anguish. Trying her best to smile at him, she said, "You really do understand, don't you?"

A wry grin twisted his lips. "Of course I understand. And if you want to stay here in El Paso for the next three weeks, I'll call Conall and have him fill in at the barn for me."

"No! Absolutely not!" she said emphatically. "You need to be there. I need to be there. And I can't rest unless I'm near the barn to make sure everything is going okay before—" She started to say "the Oaks," but caught herself. Liam was already getting the idea that she was overly obsessed with Black Dahlia and the race. She didn't want to add to his suspicions and have him plying her with more questions. Right now she felt good about the filly. She even had an excellent shot at winning. If that happened Liam would never have to know about the dire weight her father had thrown on her. "Before the baby arrives," she finally finished.

"Well, if that's the way you feel, then you have no choice but to have the baby there," he said.

She stood on the bottom step of the examining table and Liam helped her down to the floor.

"Are you okay with that?" she asked him. "This is your baby, too."

"As long as you and the baby are well cared for and that you're near your doctor whenever you go into labor is all that matters to me," he said gently.

"Thank you," she said, then smiled and squeezed his hand. "Now can we go get some lunch? I'm starving."

Later that afternoon, as Liam drove their rented truck across Desert End land on way to the ranch house, it was clear that his wife was lost in her own thoughts. From the moment they'd entered the ranch property, she'd gone rather quiet. Whenever she wasn't staring out at the rocky outcrops jutting from the low mountains and the sage dotted fields around them, she was blinking and swallowing as if she was fighting back a wall of emotions.

Kitty had never discussed her ranch with him that much. But from the few comments she made now and then, he could tell it meant the world to her. Today he'd expected her to be displaying happiness to be visiting her childhood home, but she appeared to be anything but joyful. He understood that pregnancy was causing an overload of hormones to dally with her moods, but this seemed much more than that and he could only wonder if her woeful frame of mind had anything to do with him.

"The ranch looks beautiful," Liam remarked as he glanced over at her pensive face. "Aren't you glad to see it again?"

"I'm always glad to see the ranch," she answered, then let out a long breath. "But it's—well, not quite the same with Dad not here."

"Yeah," he said softly. "I know."

Spying a wide spot on the dirt road, he suddenly pulled the truck to one side and killed the engine.

Rising up in her seat, Kitty looked at him with surprise. "Why are we stopping here?"

He shot her a clever smile then opened the lid on the console. "I was going to give you this later tonight. After supper. But I think now is a better time."

While he pulled a small package from the storage compartment, she squared around on the seat. "Give me something? When did you put that in there?"

Liam chuckled. "I can be sneaky when I need to be." From a small silver-and-white-striped sack, he pulled out a flat box covered with blue velvet and handed it to her. "I hope you like it. I'm not— Well, I never was much for buying gifts. Especially gifts for women. But you can always return it for something else."

Disbelief puckered her forehead as she cradled the box in her hands. "This is not my birthday and it's not a holiday."

"No. But I can still give my wife something, can't I?"

Nodding, she slowly opened the box to reveal a pin crafted in the shape of a racehorse carrying a jockey. The piece of jewelry was very detailed and no doubt had been very pricey to have made. The horse itself was paved with diamonds, while its black saddle towel appeared to be formed from rows of onyx. The jockey's brown and yellow silks were the exact replica of Desert End colors complete with a tiny DE on the back.

"In case you're wondering, the brown and yellow stones are topaz and citrine."

"Liam, it's exquisite," she said in a voice just slightly above a whisper. "I love it!" Suddenly galvanized with excitement, she thrust the box at him. "Pin it on me, would you, please."

Smiling indulgently, he asked, "Now? You don't want to wait until we get to the ranch where you can look in the mirror?"

"Right now!" she insisted with a bubbly laugh. "I might never take it off!"

After lifting the pin from its bed, he fastened it to the left shoulder of her blouse. The little horse and rider glittered against the blue fabric and the smile on Kitty's face as she gazed down at it made Liam feel as if he was on top of the world. To make her happy made him happy. It was as simple as that.

"It's precious, Liam. You couldn't have given me anything I'd like better." Leaning forward, she slipped her arms around his neck and pressed her cheek against his. "But you still haven't told me why I'm getting a gift."

"Let's just say—for being my wife," he murmured as he pressed his lips to her temple. She smelled sweet and sultry and as he nuzzled her soft hair, he knew with certainty that he could never go back to living his life without this woman. She filled up the holes in him. She made each day unique and special.

He couldn't say what she wanted to hear—that he loved her. Maybe because he was too much of a coward, too afraid that once he spoke the words everything would crumble and be swept away from him. He realized his fears weren't reasonable, but they were inside him just the same. Now he was hoping the pin and being by her side would show her that she was special to him, that he respected her greatly.

* * *

Later that evening, after a dinner that Coral served them, Kitty retired to her bedroom to get some much needed rest before they caught a flight back to California the next day. Since it was still early, Liam decided to walk down to the barns and look over some of the stalled horses that were presently in training.

While Willard had been alive, Liam had visited the ranch on occasions and he'd always been impressed with Desert End's facilities. The horses were supplied with the best of everything and the workers were as dedicated as those who were employed by the Diamond D stables.

He'd made his way through one of the big barns and was making his way to an adjacent building when he met an older gentleman with snow-white hair and leathery bronze skin. His wide, coarse features split into a smile when he got close enough to recognize Liam.

"Mr. Donovan! It's good to see you here on the ranch," he said as he shook Liam's outstretched hand.

"Hello, Oscar," Liam greeted the barn manager. "It's good to see you, too. How have things been going around here? Any problems?"

Even though there was a general manager for the ranch, Liam was well aware that the barn manager was the one person who kept a finger on the real heartbeat of the ranch. Oscar had held this position for probably longer than Liam had been alive and the older man was likely to remain in it until the day he died.

Tilting his head pensively to one side, Oscar answered, "Well, the drought has put a crimp on the hay supply. But I guess I can't tell you New Mexicans anything you don't already know about the hay shortage."

"It's been terrible that's for sure," Liam agreed. "But

my family has the ability to irrigate our alfalfa fields so that's helped matters."

Oscar gestured toward a row of feed buckets that were lined against the wall of the barn. "If you got a minute, let's sit," he invited.

Liam turned one of the buckets upside down and used it for a temporary seat. Oscar followed suit and once he was settled, he leaned earnestly toward Liam as though he needed to unload a heavy burden.

"Well, finding hay ain't no worry of mine. I'm not the boss around here."

"Don't sell yourself short," Liam told the other man.

Oscar pulled off a battered straw hat and swiped a hand over his thick hair. "Harrumph!" He snorted. "I've worked here for forty years, Mr. Donovan, but this has been the worst times I've ever seen on this ranch."

Empathy for the man had him reaching over and patting Oscar's shoulder. "Losing Will has been hard on everyone, Oscar. When my grandfather Donovan died our ranch just wasn't the same. Everyone was struggling to go on with their jobs and trying to do things like nothing had changed. It was hard. But with time everything gets better."

He was living proof of that, Liam thought. When he'd lost Felicia and the baby he'd truly believed his world had ended. He'd certainly never believed he'd be married again and another child soon to arrive. Most of all, he'd never thought he'd ever be able to feel this much happiness again. The idea scared him, but he was beginning to embrace it. Because he had to. Because he'd reached the point where living without Kitty was not an option.

Oscar scuffed the dirt with the toe of his boot. "It won't get better if I lose my job, Mr. Donovan."

Puzzled by the barn manager's remark, Liam studied Oscar's downcast face. "What are you talking about? You're an institution around here." He paused thoughtfully before he asked, "Is someone causing you trouble? Threatening to fire you? If they are I'll talk with Kitty about it. She'll take care of things for you."

Oscar's mouth pressed to a grim line as he stared across the way at a paddock full of yearlings. "Don't bother Miss Kitty. She has her own troubles."

Liam frowned at the man's evasive answer. "She doesn't have too many for you, Oscar. She always speaks of you with great fondness. And I know that she's grateful for the job that you do."

"Yes, sir. But—" He turned his attention back to Liam and this time his features were wrinkled with anguish. "I'm not supposed to say nothing about this, Mr. Donovan. Only a few of us folks around here know what's going on. And we don't want to talk about it. But the ones of us that do know, well, we're scared. Not just for us, but for Miss Kitty, too. That girl loves this place. Loves it with all her heart. What's it gonna do to her if she loses it? It'd be a damned shame, that's what!" He swung his head miserably. "I never thought the old man could do such a thing—especially to his own daughter. She was always so good to him and loved him so much. And this is how the bastard repays her. Just goes to show you that you never really know a person."

Totally stunned, Liam stared at the older man. "Oscar, I'm afraid that I've lost you. What's this about Will and Kitty? Why would she be about to lose this place? She's winning at the track and she's gaining horses in her barn, not losing them." And most of all, she'd not said a word about any of this to Liam, he thought uneasily. Had she been keeping something this important from him?

His thoughts spinning, he waited for the barn manager to explain.

"We all know she's been winning. We watch and keep up with all the track news. And damned right we should. It's our livelihood, too." He trained a squinted eye at Liam. "She never told you anything about the old man's will?"

Liam shook his head, while hating to admit the fact that his wife wasn't sharing important things with him. "The ranch and its holdings are her business. A few months ago, after Will died, I'd heard that all of it, except for a specified amount of money to Owen, had gone to Kitty and she's never told me any differently."

"Oh. Well—" He shook his head then, closing his eyes, pinched the bridge of his nose. "Like I said, I shouldn't be sayin' anything. Kitty didn't want it known and she's not the one who spilled the beans. She don't want people worryin' and I think she was hurt and embarrassed by what the old man had done to her. 'Course, Owen couldn't keep his mouth shut."

Desperate now for the barn manager to get to the point, Liam very nearly reached over and shook his shoulder. "But what has Willard done, Oscar? Tell me."

He drew in a long breath and let it out. "The Oaks at Hollywood. She's gotta win that race or at least place second. If she don't, the ranch is gonna go to Mr. Owen. And we all know what he'll do with it. Sell it so fast our heads will all spin. He's already strutted through the barns like he owns the place and warning that we'd all better start looking for other jobs. 'Cause there's no way in hell he'd ever give Kitty the chance to buy the place back. No, he's got a mean streak in him. Just like his daddy had."

Liam felt physically ill as the whirling in his head was quickly falling into place. Kitty working herself to the point of exhaustion. Her obsession with Black Dahlia and

the Oaks. Her order to Clayton to keep someone posted
at the filly's stall at all times. She had to win the race!
Otherwise she was going to lose this ranch, the horses,
everything she'd helped her father amass! It was incredible. She'd been carrying the heavy burden of Willard's
will right along with the baby. Oh, God, why hadn't she
told him? Did she mistrust him? Or did she—

Liam's thoughts came to a screeching halt as another
notion hit him and suddenly Kitty's words were ringing
in his head with bell-like clarity.

*If the baby comes during the Oaks, you will take over
for me, won't you? This race is so important to me. I need
your help, Liam. Clayton doesn't have your experience.
You're royalty around the tracks. Will you help me with
Dahlia?*

As Liam continued to stare in disbelief at Oscar, the
snippets of conversation tumbled over and over in his mind
until he thought his head was going to explode. Kitty was
using him. That much was plain and simple. Willard, the
man he'd befriended and loved, had turned out to be an
unfeeling son of a bitch. And his son, Owen, was apparently no better. Oh, God, and now his baby was coming
from the Cartwright family. Liam wanted to scream and
punch someone in the face.

"I—I didn't know," Liam said stiffly, then quickly rose
to his feet. "But I find it damned hard to believe that Willard has done this. He was my friend. A good man."

Rising up from his makeshift seat, Oscar cast Liam a
rueful glance. "Everybody around here thought the same
thing, too. That's what I mean, Mr. Donovan. Sometimes
a person just isn't what you think they are."

Liam heaved out a heavy breath. "Thank you for telling me, Oscar. And don't worry. I'm going to look into
all of this."

As Liam started to walk away, the other man called out to him. "Don't let Miss Kitty know that I'm the one who spilled the beans. She'll fire me for sure."

"She won't hear it from me," Liam grimly assured him.

But she was going to hear plenty of other things from him, Liam thought sickly. And he wasn't going to wait about telling her just what he thought of her!

Kitty had gotten up from her short nap and was washing her face at the bathroom sink when she heard Liam come into the bedroom.

"I'm in here, Liam," she called to him as she patted the drops of water from her cheeks.

After hanging up the towel, she glanced around to see him standing in the open doorway. A strange look was on his face, as if someone had just struck him, and her heart began to thud with uncertain dread.

"Liam? What's happened?" she asked as she hurried toward him. "Is it the horses? Is it Black Dahlia?"

His features stony, he said, "Your first concern would be about Black Dahlia, wouldn't it?"

The sarcasm in his voice stopped her short and she stared at him with confusion. "Am I supposed to understand that remark? Liam, what's wrong?"

"In a nutshell, I found out about Willard's will."

Suddenly, Kitty felt too shaky to stand and she walked past him and out to the bed where she sank weakly onto the edge of the mattress.

"How?" she asked dully. "Owen? Frankly I'm surprised he hasn't said something to you before now. He never did want me to marry you."

His features hard and ruthless, Liam strode toward her. "That's the least of our worries."

Her eyes widened. "What does that mean?"

"It means that I have a wife I can't trust!" he practically yelled at her. "I thought you married me because of the baby. Because you loved me. But none of that was true." His voice became low and vindictive. "You married me because you wanted a trainer at your beck and call. A trainer to get you through the Oaks and into the winner's circle."

The anger pulsing through her pushed away the shakiness in her knees and she shot to her feet to face him head-on. "You arrogant hypocrite! You have a megadose of nerve, don't you? You're not the only winning trainer in town! And as for love—don't try to talk about something you know nothing about!"

If anything, his face turned harder and Kitty figured if she'd had enough gumption to slap his face it would probably break her hand.

"It's obvious you'd do anything to hold on to this place. Even marry me," he practically hissed the accusation.

More angry than she could ever remember being, she shot him a cold stare. "You feel like I'm using you. Well, take a good look at me, Liam. How do you think I feel? You made it clear from the very beginning that you only married me for the baby. To you I'm nothing more than an incubator for your child. So I'm using you and you're using me. And everybody uses everybody. So get over it or get out of my life!"

"Is that the way you really feel?"

Feeling hot tears already gathering at the back of her eyes, she turned her back on him and struggled to keep them at bay. "Damned right, I do. You and this ranch can go to hell!"

Long seconds passed without any sort of reply from him and then she heard the bedroom door open and close behind her. When she finally turned and looked, Liam was gone.

Her hands covering her face, Kitty fell onto the bed, sobbing.

Kitty didn't know where Liam slept that night. And she told herself she didn't care. If her husband was more concerned about his ego than his wife's dire predicament, then she didn't need him.

But sitting beside him on the flight home and trying to keep her emotions in check hadn't been an easy thing to do. To say the trip had been strained was putting it mildly. By the time they reached their house in Westchester, Kitty was mentally and physically drained.

Even so, she quickly changed her dress for a pair of jeans and shirt and was on her way out the door when Liam called out to her.

"Where are you going now?"

Pausing, she turned back to him. "To the track. Where else? I want to check on the horses and Clayton."

He sneered. "Can't wait to see your assistant and cry on his shoulder?"

"That doesn't merit an answer," she said stiffly.

He walked closer and for a moment, as Kitty's gaze wandered over his handsome face, she prayed that something would suddenly click inside of him and make him see how much she loved and needed him. But miracles didn't happen just because a person wanted them to.

"You need to stay here and forget about that damned string of horses," he muttered. "If something happened to my baby—"

"It's my baby, too," she interrupted hotly. "And don't tell me what to do! Ever since I can remember men have been trying to run my life. First Dad, then Owen, and now

you! Well, I've had all I can take. I'm not stupid, Liam.
I'm not going to endanger the baby. Furthermore, I can
tell you right now that you've put a thousand times more
stress on me than working at the barn. So chew on that
for a while!"

Not waiting for any sort of reply, Kitty slammed out
the door and hurried to her truck.

Chapter Twelve

Three weeks later, on a late Friday evening, the bugle
call to post had already sounded and the gates were about
to crack with the first race on the card. However, Liam
wasn't over at the main track to participate as a trainer
or a fan. He was still in the training barn, going through
the motions of work.

The Oaks was only two days away now and Liam was
trying not to think about the heavy burden Kitty was facing over her father's will, or the fact that she could go into
labor at any moment. After their argument at Desert End,
she'd virtually frozen him out and he supposed he couldn't
blame her. Since the days had passed, he was beginning
to see that he'd behaved like a first-class jerk by accusing
her of marrying him to save her ranch.

Dear God, he wasn't in any position to accuse her of
anything. He'd married her solely because of the baby so
he could hardly pretend to be any better or more righteous

than she. But somewhere along the way his marriage had become more to him than simply creating a ready-made family for the child. Now, he didn't know what to do to try to fix things between them, or even if he could.

He'd told her they'd discuss their marriage once the baby had arrived and since then he'd not brought up the subject. He figured when the time came Kitty wasn't going to hesitate to tell him she wanted out of their marriage deal. She wanted love. Real love.

Isn't that what you really want, Liam? For Kitty to love you, to cherish you with all her heart? You're running scared. Running from the very thing that could make you happy.

Or the very thing that could crush him, Liam thought grimly.

Fighting back the misery in his head, he stepped out of Awesome Joe's stall and headed down the shed row toward his office. Halfway there, he caught the sound of someone calling his name.

Glancing around, he spotted a tall, dark-haired man striding quickly toward him and as he recognized his brother, a spurt of pleasure and surprise rushed through him.

"Conall! What the hell are you doing here in California?"

Conall laughed and once he was within reach, grabbed Liam up in a tight bear hug. "I heard my brother needed someone to step in and tell him how to do things. So I figured I was the man for the job."

"Bull," Liam countered with a chuckle. He'd not seen his older brother since the wedding at Desert End and Conall's strong presence was like a balm to his raw emotions. "Now tell me what you're really doing here? I hope everyone at home is okay."

"Fine. Everything is fine. Vanessa decided we needed a little summer break. And you and Kitty both have nice races scheduled for this weekend so we thought we'd come out for a little fun."

Conall had never been much of a fun type guy until about three years ago when he'd married Vanessa. Having her and the twins had changed his life for the better. But Conall was a brave man. He'd reached out and grabbed what he'd wanted. Liam wasn't quite that confident.

Liam glanced around his brother's broad shoulder. "Vanessa came with you? Is she here at the barn?"

An indulgent smile crossed Conall's face. "I left her and the twins at the mall. She wanted to buy Kitty and the baby some things before we all met up."

As glad as Liam was to have his brother here, the family visit was going to make things awkward as hell, considering the tension between him and Kitty. And in spite of Liam's effort to keep his lips spread into a smile, he could feel it quickly sliding away.

Frowning, Conall studied him with a keen eye. "Is something wrong? Is Kitty ill?"

"No," Liam answered quickly. "She was just at the doctor's office two days ago. He says everything is good and on schedule. The baby's head is down. He or she could come any day now."

"That's good." Conall placed his hand affectionately on Liam's shoulder. "So why aren't you smiling? And don't try to brush off my question. I can see the misery on your face."

Knowing he couldn't fool his brother for long, Liam jerked his head toward the end of the barn. "Let's go down to my office where we can talk in private."

Five minutes later, the two men were secluded in the

private space of Liam's office. Conall took a seat on the small couch while Liam poured them both a cup of coffee.

"We haven't made any definite plans yet," Conall said, "but Vanessa was hoping you two might join us for dinner tonight. That is, if you think you can put up with the twins. They have fairly good table manners. But they're at that age where they talk incessantly and the questions never stop."

Conall's wife, Vanessa, had unexpectedly become mother to newborn twins when the birth mother had suddenly died and left them in her care. And since Conall had lost his fertility to a childhood illness, being able to adopt the twins was an extra special miracle for the both of them. If anyone understood the deep hunger Liam felt for a child of his own, it was Conall.

Liam handed one of the coffee cups to his brother, but didn't join him on the couch. He was too restless to sit. "The twins are a joy to us. But, well, I'm not sure Kitty will want to have a family dinner. She's, uh, not too happy with me right now."

Conall's eyes narrowed shrewdly as he watched Liam sip his coffee.

"That kills you to admit that, doesn't it?" he asked.

Liam grimaced. "That's a fool question. Hell, would you want to admit that Vanessa couldn't stand the sight of you?"

"Not exactly. But I'll be the first to admit that in the beginning we had our own rocky moments. But you're the world's worst about wanting to pretend that everything is rosy."

Liam wandered aimlessly to the other side of the room and eased a hip onto the edge of his desk. "I've always been able to talk to you. You're my brother."

Conall sipped his coffee before casting Liam a droll

look. "Yeah. That much is true. Otherwise I would've never known that my ex-wife begged you to get her pregnant."

Liam let out a loud groan. "Why did you bring up that sordid ordeal? That happened years ago. And Nancy had become mentally ill. You had to be told."

Liam had hated like hell to have to be the one to inform Conall that his wife had gone off the deep end and propositioned her brother-in-law. But Conall had respected Liam for having the guts to be open and honest with him. In the end, the whole issue had drawn the two brothers closer together.

"That was one of the few times you spoke up when you needed to," Conall replied. "But most of the time you're the mute one of our family. So tell me what's wrong and we'll fix it."

Liam's lips twisted to a wry slant. "I realize you're the oldest and wisest and all that good stuff, but you're not a miracle worker, Conall."

"Are things really so bad that you need a miracle? That's hard to believe. You and Kitty seem perfect for each other."

Liam wiped a hand over his weary face. "I was beginning to think so, too. But I've made a mess of things, Conall. And everything is just so damned complicated now."

A dumbfounded expression came over Conall's face. "What things are you talking about? And what is this 'beginning to think so'? Weren't you sure about your feelings for the woman before you ever married her?"

Liam could feel a red flush creep over his face. "I was sure I wanted her. And I was sure I wanted our baby to have married parents."

Conall stared at him with a mixture of disgust and

disbelief. "That's all? What about love? Don't you love Kitty?"

Rolling his eyes toward the ceiling, Liam groaned. "Look, Conall, I need to explain—the baby was conceived because of a one-night stand. Kitty and I— Well, we didn't have anything serious going on between us."

Conall appeared shocked and deflated and Liam grunted with cynical humor. "What the hell is wrong with you? Since when have you gotten so righteous that you want to judge me for having sex with a woman?"

"Damn it, Liam, I'm not judging you! I'm just thinking that you're not a one-night stand kind of guy. You never were and you aren't now. So don't try to tell me that you took Kitty to bed without having any feelings for her!"

Gripping his coffee cup with both hands, Liam stared at his brother while he thought back to that night the baby was conceived. Had he felt more than just physical attraction for Kitty then? At the time he'd told himself it was only sex, but that idea had always gnawed at him and dared him to take a deeper look at his feelings. But he'd been afraid to take that look. Afraid he might actually see a thread of love wound through them.

Sighing heavily, he said, "I first met Kitty when she was only seventeen. I was married to Felicia at the time and, to me, Kitty was just Willard's child, nothing more. Then Felicia was killed and for years after that the idea of connecting with any female was an obscene thought."

"But then you started noticing Kitty and something changed," Conall went on for him.

Liam looked down at the strong brown liquid in his cup. "Yes. And I guess—oh, hell, Conall—after that night with Kitty everything seemed to change. I couldn't stop thinking about her any more than I could stop wanting to see her again."

"Sounds to me like you'd already fallen in love with her," Conall surmised.

Liam could feel the blood draining from his face as a fatal acceptance washed over him. How easy it was for Conall to speak those words, Liam thought miserably, when he'd been fighting against them for months, afraid that if he spoke them, his world would fall apart. He realized his resistance hadn't made good sense, but understanding that hadn't made it any easier to deal with.

"Conall, I don't want to love Kitty. I never wanted to fall in love with her."

"Why? Because you feel guilty about Felicia?"

Liam looked across the room at his brother. "No. Felicia was a practical person. She would have been the first person to want me to get married again. But what I feel for Kitty—it's so different. Felicia and I had a quiet, comfortable relationship. This thing with Kitty is wild and it's grabbed me so hard that I can't think straight."

Grinning wryly, Conall said, "Vanessa still makes me feel that way. And I expect she will until the day I die. That's the way love is supposed to be."

"Love! Damn it, Conall, I loved Felicia and you know what losing her and the baby did to me. I don't want to hurt like that again. I don't want to go through years of feeling dead. If I lose Kitty—"

"Forget about losing, Liam!" Conall swiftly interrupted. "It's time you started concentrating on living. Last fall you would've never known the joy of winning a Breeder's Cup championship race with Kate's Kitten if you'd been so afraid of losing that you'd not entered the filly in the first place. It's the same way with love and marriage. It's obvious as hell to me that you love Kitty. You need to grab on to her and never let go. If you don't throw everything into the ring, you've already lost."

Liam raked both hands through his hair. "I'm afraid I have already lost," he muttered miserably. "She thinks I only married her because of the baby. And I never told her any differently. Then about three weeks ago I found out quite by accident that Willard left a stipulation in his will. If Kitty doesn't win the Oaks, Desert End and all its holdings will go to her brother, Owen."

Conall sat straight up and scooted to the edge of his seat. "The hell you say!"

"That's right. I find it hard to believe the old man could have done such a thing to his daughter. But it's true. And I was— Well, I reacted badly to the whole thing. Mainly because she kept the problem from me."

Conall shook his head with stunned disbelief. "Oh, poor Kitty. My God, I can't imagine the strain she's been under. What she must be going through!" His gaze settled perceptively on Liam. "You say you reacted badly—what—"

"I jumped to conclusions and we ended up having a horrible row." Pushing himself off the desk, Liam walked over to his brother. "I accused her of marrying me so that she'd have an experienced trainer to help her win the Oaks and keep her home."

Conall's frown was full of disappointment and Liam realized he couldn't feel any lower than he did at this moment.

"I hope she told you what a jerk you are," Conall said.

Liam heaved out a heavy breath. "More or less. And now, I expect that once the baby is born she'll ask for a divorce."

"I'm assuming that you don't want that to happen."

"Hell, no! I can't lose her, Conall. I just can't. And this is not about the baby. Kitty is a fair woman. I'm certain she'd agree to equal custody. I'm not concerned about that issue. This is just about my wife and how nothing would matter to me if I didn't have her in my life."

"If that's the case, then you'd better get on your knees and do some confessing."

Liam's throat was suddenly so tight his next words came out in a hoarse whisper. "I'm not so sure that getting on my knees will soften her heart toward me."

"Don't worry about the knees, Liam. It's what comes out of your mouth that's most important." Conall rose to his feet and slapped a reassuring hand on Liam's shoulder. "Where is Kitty now? At home?"

Seeing that it was already dark, his wife should be home. But lately, she'd been staying here at the track later and later. To avoid him, no doubt.

"She's probably still here in the barn," Liam answered, then shrugged. "She doesn't always inform me whenever she's going home."

"That bad, huh?"

"Yeah. That bad."

"Then you'd better go find her."

Liam stared at him in wonder and his heart began to thud with a mixture of hope and dread. "You mean now?"

"I mean right this instant!"

"But you just got here and—"

Conall shoved Liam's shoulder in the direction of the door. "I'll be here for several days. We'll have plenty of time to get together. All of us. As a family."

"Oh, God, I hope you're right." At the door, he turned back and gave Conall a tight hug. "Thanks, brother."

His voice rough with emotion, Conall said, "Get out of here."

For the past three weeks, Kitty had purposely kept her distance from Liam. She'd driven herself to and from the track and while she was there, she remained on her end of the barn, while Liam stayed on his.

Enduring her husband's cold, detached attitude only made her feel worse about everything. Besides, it was clear their marriage, for whatever it was worth, was over. She couldn't figure why he was waiting until after the baby was born to tell her he wanted a divorce. It was clearly evident to Kitty that he no longer wanted to be her husband.

She was surprised he'd not taken to staying nights at his office. But she supposed he'd chosen not to because it was so close to her delivery. He wouldn't want to be away from the house in case she did go into labor. Making sure the baby arrived safely was the utmost important thing to him and she was very glad that he loved the child she was carrying. Her problem was that he couldn't bring himself to extend that feeling toward its mother.

She released a weary sigh as she slowly made her way to Dahlia's stall. Loving Liam as she did was useless. She needed to move on and find someone who could truly love her in return. But she didn't want someone else. She wanted Liam.

At Dahlia's door, Maryann, one of Kitty's hot walkers, was taking a shift at guarding Dahlia's stall. The young woman was sitting in a lawn chair, reading a book. Since the main lights in the barn had been dimmed more than an hour ago, Maryann was using a penlight to see the text. Kitty's heart went out to her.

"Maryann, go take a break," she told the young woman. "I'll stay with Dahlia for a while."

Reaching for a tote bag near the leg of her chair, she shoved the book inside it. "Are you sure, Miss Kitty? It's getting late. I thought you'd already be headed home."

"I'm just now winding up a very busy day," Kitty explained. And she didn't want to go home. It hurt too much to be physically under the same roof with Liam but not really having him with her in spirit. So she stayed at the track as much as possible and tried to pretend to everyone that she was happy. "Don't worry about it. Go take a break and I'll call you whenever I need to leave."

Inside the stall she found Dahlia bedded down on the clean straw that was spread several inches deep over the concrete flooring. Not wanting to disturb the filly, Kitty gently eased down on the bedding next to the horse's head.

Gently stroking the side of Dahlia's cheeks, she said, "You're a tired, sleepy girl. You've been working hard. But you'll soon get a nice deserved rest, I promise."

The horse groaned softly as though she understood what her mistress was saying. The reaction put a wan smile on Kitty's face.

"This has been a long, hard journey for both of us," Kitty went on. "I'm sure much harder for you than for me. I want you to know how proud I am of you, my Dahlia. You've given me everything I asked of you and more. And Sunday when you leave that gate I know you'll be running with your heart. There're a lot of folks counting on you. Folks that might lose their homes and jobs if you don't win. But they all love you and know that you'll do your best, too. And no matter what happens in the Oaks, I want you to remember that I'll still love you. And I'll be very, very proud of you, too."

Kitty went quiet for a few moments and even though Dahlia's eyes were shut, the slight twitch of the filly's ear told her that she was awake and listening to her voice.

After stroking her for a few more minutes, Kitty spoke again. "I've been thinking a lot here, lately. And I'm not sure what's going to happen to you and me once this race is over, Dahlia. We might not have a home to go to. And someone might try to take you away from me." She stopped and swallowed hard as tears began to pour from her eyes. "But I'm not going to let them. No matter what. You and the other horses are my children. I'll keep you somehow, someway—because I love you all."

She wiped a stream of tears from her cheeks then stared down at her hand in the muted light filtering through the stall. Even in the shadows her wedding band glinted against her skin and she gently touched the heavy gold the same way she used to touch Liam's face.

"Some people would call me silly for saying that. But those people don't understand what it means to love. Like Liam—I tried to tell him, show him how much I loved him. But it didn't mean anything to him. That's the way it is when your love isn't returned. Now I'm going to have his baby and I thank God for that. It's the only bright star I have to hang on to. The baby and you. Liam has deserted us, but—"

"Liam hasn't deserted you. I'm right here. I'll always be right here."

The sound of her husband's voice shocked her and her head jerked around as her eyes searched the semidarkness of the stall.

"Where—where did you come from?" she asked dazedly.

He entered the stall and safely latched the gate behind him. "If you're wondering whether I was eavesdropping, I confess. I'm guilty."

Her face flamed with embarrassment. "Oh. I didn't realize anyone was around. Especially you."

He walked over to where she sat and reached a hand down to her. Her heart beating hard in her chest, she placed her hand in his and allowed him to help her to her feet.

Once she was standing, she smoothed her loose shirt

over her belly. For some reason this evening the baby had quit all of its kicking, as though it was either sleeping or allowing her to rest. Now she felt it give her a little nudge in the ribs, right beneath her heart.

"I should apologize for not letting you know I was listening. But I'm not going to. I'm glad I heard what was in your heart, Kitty."

Tilting her head back, she stared at him in wonder. "Why?"

He moved closer, and as his hands gently delved into her hair, she felt as though she was going to wilt right into his arms.

"Because now I really understand what it all means, my darling. You. Me. The baby. Your ranch and horses." With a choked groan he pulled her tightly against him and buried his face in the crook of her neck. "Oh, Kitty, forgive me. I've been such a coward. I thought I could stop myself from loving you. But I can't. I love you more than anything. Anything."

She eased her head back far enough to look into his face and what she saw in his eyes stunned her. "Liam— I don't understand. You accused me of using you to save my ranch. You said you'd never love any woman. I—"

"I was wrong about all of that. In fact, I think I've been wrong for several years now."

Everything he was saying was almost too much for her to take in and though she wanted to shout with happiness, she was afraid to let herself believe what she was hearing. "What does that mean?"

"It means that all those years I told myself that you were just the pretty daughter of a good friend, I was falling in love with you. And that night we made the baby I could feel it in my heart. But then you said you wanted to keep our relationship as just friends, so I tamped all those feelings down and convinced myself that your friendship was all that I needed."

Kitty shook her head ruefully. "Oh, Liam, I only said that to save face. Because I knew you'd only gone to bed with me to have sex. And you'd already told Dad that you didn't want to seriously date me." ·

His head jerked up with surprise. "You knew about that?"

"He told me. During one of those times we were fighting about me finding a husband. You see, over the years, Dad tried to pick out several suitors for me. One even presented me with an engagement ring. And I infuriated Dad by throwing the ring back in the guy's face. He knew that I liked you and I guess it made him feel good to rub in the fact that Liam Donovan wasn't interested in the likes of Kitty Cartwright."

"I never realized your father could be so vindictive," he said ruefully.

Kitty sighed. "He wasn't vindictive. He wanted to control me. Just like he wanted to control everyone that he loved. Now I guess you could say he's still trying to control me from the grave."

His fingertips gently caressed her cheek. "At the time your father asked me about courting you, I wasn't ready for any kind of dating. Felicia hadn't been dead that long and I was still trying to get my feet back under me. That's why I told him I wasn't interested. But later, I began to find everything about you interesting." Bending his head, he placed kisses on her forehead, cheeks and finally her lips. "You've been my wife in name for several months now, Kitty. But I want you to be my wife in every sense of the word. I love you. I don't want to live without you."

Behind her she could hear Black Dahlia begin to stir and Kitty looked around just as the filly stood on her feet.

And then, as though the horse understood that prompting was needed, she used her nose to nudge Kitty even closer to Liam.

Laughing, Kitty wrapped her arms tightly around his waist. "It appears that Dahlia knows I don't want to live without you, either."

Chuckling with her, Liam lowered his mouth to Kitty's and kissed her for long moments, a kiss that swept away the fears of the past and carried them straight into their future together.

"Kitty, this thing with your father's will...if Dahlia doesn't win, I—"

"She will win. I feel it inside," she said, placing a hand over the region of her heart.

"I have the same feeling. Not just from a trainer's standpoint, but as your husband," he agreed. "But if she doesn't, I'll help you fight this thing. I won't let you lose Desert End or the horses. Even if I have to knock Owen on his ass."

Rising up on her tiptoes, Kitty pressed another kiss on his lips. "At this moment, Liam, I can truly say that no matter what happens, I'll be happy. Just as long as I have you and our baby. We can always buy another ranch and more horses."

Dahlia chose that moment to nicker softly and both Kitty and Liam turned around to look at the filly.

"Okay, okay. We'll make sure we have you, too," Kitty told the horse.

"Tell her good-night," Liam urged. "I have something out here I want to give you."

Kitty waited until she'd kissed the filly's nose and then followed Liam out of the stall before she voiced her curiosity. "What is it? You just gave me a piece of expensive jewelry."

"This is something totally different." Reaching down, he picked up a flat box from the chair where Maryann had been sitting. "I've kept this all these years and now I hope you'll put it to use."

He handed her the box and she opened the lid to find a book covered with padded fabric of pale blue. As she lifted it from the bed of tissue paper he said in a husky voice, "My mother gave me this journal when she learned that Felicia was pregnant. She wanted me to document the first year of my child's life so that I would always be able to relive the special moments. It's only right that you have it now."

Tears suddenly clogged her throat and for long moments she was too touched to speak. "Oh, Liam, this is—" Lost for words to explain how she was feeling, Kitty shook her head. "I love you and our baby. So much."

"Let's go home," he said simply.

Kitty agreed and after she'd carefully returned the journal to its box and called Maryann back to the stall to stand post, they started out of the training barn.

They were on the verge of exiting the building when Kitty suddenly realized she'd forgotten to collect her purse from her office.

"I have to go back for it, Liam," she insisted. "I'll need my keys and wallet."

"All right," he told her. "But there's no need in you making the long walk with me. Wait here at the door and I'll be right back."

Kitty nodded and then just as he started to walk away, a sharp pain struck the side of her stomach, causing her to bend over and cry out.

"Liam! Wait!"

Rushing back to her, he grabbed her by the arm. "Kitty! What's wrong? Is it the baby?"

"I think so!"

Not waiting to ask more questions, Liam swept her up in his arms. "I've got to get you to the hospital before our Texas baby is born in a training barn!"

Chapter Thirteen

Five hours later, Liam was standing at his wife's side, gripping her hand as she pushed their new son into the world.

The baby weighed nearly eight pounds and squalled at the top of his lungs while the nurses cleaned and wrapped him in a tiny blue blanket.

"He looks and sounds like a healthy one," the doctor proudly announced as he finished the last of his ministrations to Kitty.

Full of love and great relief, Liam bent his head and pressed a kiss to his wife's damp forehead. "We have a son, my darling. Thank you for him. Thank you for loving me."

Tears slipped from the corners of her eyes and as he tenderly wiped them away, Kitty tried to laugh through her weariness.

"Are you happy that he's a boy?"

"I would have been thrilled either way." Although the labor had been relatively short, the intensity of the pains had drained her and now as she looked up at him with sleepy blue eyes, he was amazed by her courage and strength. He was amazed that he'd found such a remarkable woman to love him.

"Good," she said softly. "Maybe the next one will be a girl."

Chuckling, he stroked a finger against her pale cheek. "Next one?"

A drowsy smile tilted the corners of her mouth. "We're only just beginning, my darling."

Liam had just finished placing a kiss on her lips when a nurse appeared at the side of the delivery table. The baby was cradled in the woman's arms.

"We need to put him in the incubator and let him get warm before you two start handling him. But I thought you might want to take a tiny peek first," she said with an understanding smile.

Lowering the baby so that Kitty could also get a view, the nurse pulled back the corner of blanket covering the baby's face. And as Liam studied the tiny nose and bow-shaped lips, the squinted eyes and red mottled skin, he knew he'd never gazed on anything more beautiful or precious.

Tears sprouted to his eyes, but he didn't attempt to stop them. For a long time he'd believed his life was over. But as Kitty had just said, they were just now beginning and all he could see ahead of him was love.

"Mmm. Lucky me. He looks just like his daddy," Kitty said dreamily.

Liam blushed, and the nurse laughed.

"She's delirious," Liam explained his wife's comment.

Giving Liam a saucy wink, the nurse flipped the blanket back over the baby's face and started out of the room.

As she shouldered her way through a swinging door, she called back, "Your wife isn't delirious, Mr. Donovan. She's in love."

By Sunday afternoon, Kitty and the baby were released from the hospital. As soon as Liam got them safely ensconced at home, he and Conall raced to the track in order to help Clayton get Black Dahlia saddled and prepared for the big race.

"Your nerves must be on the edge of exploding," Vanessa said to her as the other woman switched on the television and tuned it to the horse-racing channel. "Bringing home a newborn baby, the first one at that, and now the race. I'll admit, Kitty, I could never be as calm as you are right now."

Propped in a partially reclined position on the couch, Kitty glanced over at the white bassinet sitting only inches away from her left shoulder. The baby was asleep, but she could hardly tear her eyes from his perfect little face. They had decided to name him Corey Arthur after Liam's late Grandfather Donovan, but Liam had already given him the nickname of Jock and though Kitty pretended to hate the moniker she'd found herself calling the baby by that name.

"Believe me, if you saw my insides you could see they were jumping up and down with nerves." Touching the sparkly horse and jockey she'd pinned to her blouse, she smiled at her sister-in-law. "I'm so glad you're here with me, Vanessa. I've never had much of a chance to be around babies, especially newborns. And you had two at once. You're an expert on baby advice."

Vanessa laughed. "No one is ever an expert on babies or children. They're all different. Even my twins are different." She sat down in a stuffed armchair a few feet away from Kitty. "I'm just wondering how Conall thinks he's going to manage them at the track. Especially when Michael runs one way and Maria runs the other. I'm guessing before the afternoon is over he'll have Liv and Edie helping him."

Kitty nodded. "Yes, thank God for Liam's hot walkers. Even when Liam and I were at odds, the two women were kind enough to search me out every day and offer to do anything that I needed done."

Vanessa smiled at her. "The Diamond D has very special people working for them. But then so does Desert End. Are you and Liam planning on making it your permanent home?"

Kitty released a nervous laugh. "We've not talked about it yet. And anything I say would be premature. In less than two hours the ranch might not be mine anymore."

Vanessa shook her head. "Don't say that! Conall watched the video of Dahlia's last work. He said she was floating over the ground. He truly believes she'll win."

Glad to have her attention slightly diverted from her coiled nerves, Kitty looked curiously at her sister-in-law. "Liam talks more about Conall than he does any of his other siblings and he tells me that your husband is quite a horseman in his own right."

Smiling proudly, Vanessa nodded. "He is. When he was in his teens he used to gallop for his family barn. And he's admitted that training is his first love. But because he has a business degree, his father always expected him to manage the ranch."

"Oh. That must make him feel sort of caged."

"I think it did at one time. But that's about to change. Their cousin Clancy has moved to New Mexico from Kentucky and he's going to take over the managing job so that Conall will be free to help Liam."

"Oh, that's great news!"

"Yes, I think that's one of the reasons Conall wanted to come out here this weekend. So he could tell Liam in person about all their new plans." The other woman got to her feet and peered over the basinet at her new nephew. "We didn't know we were arriving just in time for Corey's birth."

A small smile touched Kitty's lips. "It's nice to have family here. I only wish—"

"That your brother cared enough to acknowledge you and the baby?" Vanessa asked knowingly.

Kitty sighed. "Liam called him with the news, but he never really told me how my brother reacted. I..."

Her words trailed off as the doorbell suddenly rang. "Who in the world could that be? Everyone we know is at the track right now."

"I'll go see," Vanessa assured her.

The woman disappeared into a small foyer only to return moments later with Owen following her. Kitty stared in shock at her brother who had his arms filled with flowers and balloons and a huge teddy bear.

"Owen!" She rose to her feet to greet him. "What are you doing here?"

He walked straight to Kitty and after handing her the flowers, pressed a kiss on her cheek. "I'm here to see my sister and new nephew," he explained.

"Aren't you more concerned about who wins the Oaks?"

Ignoring Kitty's pointed question, Owen propped the brown-and-white teddy bear against the leg of the bassinet, then bent over for a closer look at the baby.

Vanessa awkwardly cleared her throat. "If you two will excuse me, I'll go make coffee."

As the other woman left the room, Kitty realized her legs were trembling and she sank onto the couch while her brother gazed at his new nephew.

"The baby looks like Liam," he remarked. "Congratulations, sis." Turning away from the bassinet, he looked at Kitty. "As for the Oaks, I want you to win it, Kit."

Kitty's first instinct was to hurl a sarcastic remark back at him, but as silent seconds ticked by, she could see he was actually being sincere.

Stunned, she stared at him. "Seriously?"

Grinning now, he removed his cowboy hat and sat a few inches away from her feet. "I'll sit here so you can go ahead and kick me. I realize I deserve it."

With a slight shake of her head, Kitty said, "I don't understand any of this, Owen. You never wanted for me to—"

He held up a hand before she could start. "Look, Kitty, I don't expect you to understand any of this. I don't even expect you to believe me or forgive me for the pain I've put you through. I'm just now getting it all settled in my own mind."

"And when did this change of heart happen?" she asked skeptically.

He shrugged. "I think that night we last saw each other at Desert End. You said something that I couldn't get out of my mind and it began to eat on me."

"Really? What was it? That you had the same controlling personality that Dad had?"

"That wasn't it. Although, I will admit that I am a bit of a control freak."

He must have expected her to let out a mocking howl at

that because he seemed surprised when she simply stared at him.

"Just a tad," she finally agreed.

He rubbed his palms against his thighs as though he was nervous. The idea was more than a bit shocking. From the time they were children until now, she'd never seen Owen nervous. He'd always been sure of himself, almost to the point of arrogance. This was definitely a different Owen sitting next to her.

His gaze slipped away from her and over to the picture window that framed a view of the front yard. "What really got to me," he said in a low, strained voice, "was when you said that you would never tell me what sort of job I should have. I love being a sheriff's deputy. If you told me my job wasn't good for me—that would really hurt. I thought about that long and hard, Kitty. And slowly I began to see I was hurting you by refusing to accept the career you'd chosen for yourself."

Amazed that her brother was actually displaying some understanding, she said, "Everyone should have the right to make their own choices."

His forehead puckered with a remorseful frown. "Ever since Dad died, I've begun to see that I'm more like him than I care to admit." He looked at her and his eyes implored her to understand. "When Liam called me with news about the baby something happened to me. And all I could think about was the days and months I let go by without connecting with you. This should have been a very special time in your life—for mine, too. I feel like a bastard for ruining it."

"You haven't ruined anything," she assured him, then in a softer voice added, "Owen, these past few years, since I started traveling with Dad, you became less and less a part of the family. I thought it was because you resented my close relationship with him."

"I suppose you could say I did resent it. I've always felt left out—I was never good with horses and you were. You shared so much with Dad. Then after he died I thought you'd turn to me. Instead, you came out here to California to train, and married Liam. After that it was pretty clear you weren't going to sit around and wait for me to become a part of the family again. I felt like you'd completely turned your back on me. That's why I thought if I threatened to sell the ranch away from you that you'd come running back to Texas and turn to me for help."

"That was selfish and stupid, Owen. I've always been your sister and that will never change, no matter what I'm doing or where I'm living. You'll always be welcome in my home and I hope I'll always be welcome in yours. And no matter what our jobs are or where we live, we can remain close."

He looked totally humbled and Kitty's heart suddenly swelled with love and forgiveness.

"I'm amazed you can feel that way after all the horrible threats I made."

Scooting closer, she laid her hand on his arm. "Look, I still love Dad even though that will of his has put me through hell. And I still love you in spite of all those ugly words. I said a few to you, too. So we'll consider them canceled and forgotten."

"I think I need to take you to the doctor," he said with a grin. "You're obviously suffering from an enlarged heart."

Smiling through her tears, she held her arms out to him. "Come here."

Brother and sister were hugging just as Vanessa entered the room carrying a tray with coffee and thick slices of cake.

"Looks like I'm just in time to celebrate," she announced.

Kitty eased back from him and laughed. "I couldn't agree more."

Later that night the house was full of family and friends. Piles of delicious food hastily purchased from a nearby deli were being consumed, while happy toasts were being made with glasses of chilled champagne. The American Oaks was now history and Black Dahlia's name would be written next to the great fillies that had won the prestigious race for the past sixty-seven years before her.

Seeing her fly across the finish line nearly two lengths ahead of her nearest competitor seemed almost surreal after the mounting pressure Kitty had been living under these past few months. For a few seconds she'd simply stared in shock at the image on the television screen, even as the track announcer was shouting Dahlia's name with wild excitement. And then Kitty began to cry and laugh at the same time. She'd won. She'd won! Not only the race, but she'd won her husband's love and her brother's respect. And she'd been monumentally blessed with a child. The joy of it all had almost been too much for her to bear.

Now, hours later, with the party still going full force, she'd taken the baby to the bedroom and lay down to catch a few minutes of rest.

She had Corey Arthur snuggled to her side and was gazing wondrously at his sleeping face when Liam entered the room. As he sat on the edge of the bed only inches away from her and the baby, she smiled up at him.

"The party still going on?" she asked.

"I'm beginning to think it might last all night. But don't worry, I'll make them hold down the noise or kick them out and send them to the nearest bar," he joked.

"Oh, Liam, I don't think I could be any happier than I am right now."

His expression turned serious as he leaned over and kissed her lips. "And I have never been happier, either, Kitty. We make a great team, don't we?"

She cupped her palm against the side of his face. "The best."

He kissed her again then glanced down at his son. "My little Texas baby is sleeping peacefully, but I'd love to hold him."

"I'm sure he'd love to feel his daddy's strong arms around him," Kitty assured him.

Smiling now, Liam carefully scooped up the sleeping baby. "Come here, little Jock, and let me tell you what it's like to train thoroughbred racehorses."

"Liam!" she laughingly scolded again. "That's not our son's name!"

His fingers gently smoothed over the baby's dark brown hair. "No. But that's the name that comes to me whenever I look at him."

"If you hang that nickname on him now he'll have it for the rest of his life," she warned him.

Liam chuckled. "Look at his hands. He's going to be a big guy like your father was. If he doesn't want to be called Jock, he'll get the point over. We'll let him make the choice as to what name he wants to go by."

"Mmm. Choices. I wonder if Dad can see that I made the right choice in marrying you?"

Liam's gaze was full of love as he looked at his wife. "He'd probably say you can prove that to me in fifty years."

Kitty rested her cheek against his strong shoulder. "In fifty years I'll still be able to say I made the right choice."

* * *

Nearly six months later snow was falling on a cold Christmas Eve. Inside the massive Diamond D ranch house, the staff was bustling with party preparations and the females in the family were already dressing for the event. The children, those who were old enough to understand that Santa Claus was soon coming, repeatedly peered out the windows in hopes they'd spot a sleigh flying across the snowy sky.

Liam and Kitty, along with their son, had driven over from Desert End, to join in the merrymaking with the whole Donovan gang. And to Kitty's utter surprise, Owen had accepted an invitation to join them. He'd even managed to manipulate his work schedule in order to spend Christmas Day with his family.

Since the day of the Oaks, Kitty's life had changed and each day that passed was like a new and bright adventure. Jock, as he was now called by everyone, was thriving with two new teeth, a crawl that would rival Black Dahlia's speed, along with a boisterous personality, so it was apparent the nickname fit him.

With the success of the Diamond D stables on the West Coast, Conall and Liam had decided to ship even more contenders to California training barns. This meant that she and Liam were often shuffling to and fro between Desert End and Westchester. But that was a part of the job. And now that Conall and Vanessa would be joining them on the West Coast throughout the summer, she was looking ever more forward to gearing up for a new racing season.

Presently, Kitty was still hard at work, training her own horses and for the most part, she and Liam took Jock along with them to the barns every day. When occasions arose that she needed to remain at home with the baby, Clayton stepped in and carried the brunt of the workload for her.

Being a wife, mother and trainer was a balancing act for Kitty; just as it was for every woman who cherished having a family and career. But it was worth the harried moments and she wouldn't change a thing in her life.

"Kitty! Where are you?"

From the second-floor landing, Liam's voice filtered into their bedroom and she twisted around on the vanity seat to call to him through the partially open door.

"In here, Liam. I'm trying to do my hair for tonight. But Jock keeps crawling off, searching for something to get into. I've already caught him chewing on one of your boots. We might as well get him a rawhide bone to cut his teeth on," she joked.

Laughing, Liam scooped up his son and began to tickle the child's belly. From her seat in front of the dressing table, Kitty watched the playful exchange between father and son. And then she spotted the large envelope jammed beneath one arm.

"What's that? The health papers on the chestnut colt? If they don't come soon we won't be able to ship him."

"The health papers have already arrived. But this is something else. A courier delivered this for you about five minutes ago. I thought you might want to open it right away."

Shuffling the baby over to one arm, he handed Kitty the large envelope. "The return address is your lawyer in El Paso."

"Hmm. I can't think of any reason he'd be writing and sending it rush delivery." Faintly alarmed, Kitty quickly put aside her hairbrush and ripped into the correspondence.

"Oh, my," she said as she quickly scanned the first few sentences. "It's from Dad."

"Willard? What is it? An old letter the lawyer thought you might like to keep?"

"Let me see. It was written several months before he died." Her gaze momentarily left the letter to look thoughtfully at her husband. "I wonder if he sensed that death was drawing near?"

"Hard to say. He never mentioned any concerns to me. Perhaps you'll know more about that when you read it," Liam suggested.

Swallowing hard, Kitty turned her attention back to her father's bold handwriting and began to read aloud.

My dear Kitty,
Since I ordered this letter to be given to you on the first Christmas after my death, then I can no longer be with you in the flesh. But make no mistake; I will always be with you in spirit.

I suspect the trial I put you through over the past few months has left you wondering why I could ever contemplate separating you from Desert End and its horses. It's time that you learned the truth. There was never any danger of the ranch going to Owen or anyone else. A codicil was added to my initial will to make certain that Desert End would remain in your hands.

As to my reasons, I understood that upon the event of my death, a giant responsibility would fall on your shoulders and I wanted you to be certain that being a horse trainer was really the life you wanted. God knows, it's an unpredictable job with high pressures and long hours. But the rewards are immeasurable. I trust that my challenge to you has proved all of that and more. And I hope you are moving into the future with a steady hand on the reins of Desert End and all of its holdings.

This trial was not only for you, my daughter, but also for your brother, Owen. Would he step up and support his sister's efforts? Or would he choose wealth over family and his childhood home? It's my deepest wish that, during the time leading up to the Oaks, he has also learned what is most important to him and his life.

I've been a far from perfect father and you and I clashed many times down through the years. But always remember that my motives were based on love. So with all of this, my beautiful daughter, I wish you a Merry Christmas. And whenever you stand at the edge of the track and hear the thunder of pounding hooves, know that I'm always beside you, my ears listening to the same music.

Tears of amazement glazed Kitty's eyes as she lifted her gaze from the letter. "Oh, Liam—my father did truly love me."

A tender smile touched her husband's lips. "He's given you an incredible gift, my darling. One that will stay with you forever."

Rising to her feet, she went to him and circled her arms around him and the baby. "That's right," she said in a husky voice. "He's the reason that you and I met and fell in love. So in a roundabout way, he's given me you and our son. And that's the greatest gift of all."

* * * * *

REQUEST YOUR FREE BOOKS!

2 FREE NOVELS PLUS 2 FREE GIFTS!

⬦ Harlequin®

SPECIAL EDITION

Life, Love & Family

YES! Please send me 2 FREE Harlequin® Special Edition novels and my 2 FREE gifts (gifts are worth about $10). After receiving them, if I don't wish to receive any more books, I can return the shipping statement marked "cancel." If I don't cancel, I will receive 6 brand-new novels every month and be billed just $4.49 per book in the U.S. or $5.24 per book in Canada. That's a saving of at least 14% off the cover price! It's quite a bargain! Shipping and handling is just 50¢ per book in the U.S. and 75¢ per book in Canada.* I understand that accepting the 2 free books and gifts places me under no obligation to buy anything. I can always return a shipment and cancel at any time. Even if I never buy another book, the two free books and gifts are mine to keep forever.

235/335 HDN FEGF

Name _____ (PLEASE PRINT)

Address _____ Apt. #

City _____ State/Prov. _____ Zip/Postal Code

Signature (if under 18, a parent or guardian must sign)

Mail to the **Reader Service:**
IN U.S.A.: P.O. Box 1867, Buffalo, NY 14240-1867
IN CANADA: P.O. Box 609, Fort Erie, Ontario L2A 5X3

Not valid for current subscribers to Harlequin Special Edition books.

**Want to try two free books from another line?
Call 1-800-873-8635 or visit www.ReaderService.com.**

* Terms and prices subject to change without notice. Prices do not include applicable taxes. Sales tax applicable in N.Y. Canadian residents will be charged applicable taxes. Offer not valid in Quebec. This offer is limited to one order per household. All orders subject to credit approval. Credit or debit balances in a customer's account(s) may be offset by any other outstanding balance owed by or to the customer. Please allow 4 to 6 weeks for delivery. Offer available while quantities last.

Your Privacy—The Reader Service is committed to protecting your privacy. Our Privacy Policy is available online at www.ReaderService.com or upon request from the Reader Service.

We make a portion of our mailing list available to reputable third parties that offer products we believe may interest you. If you prefer that we not exchange your name with third parties, or if you wish to clarify or modify your communication preferences, please visit us at www.ReaderService.com/consumerschoice or write to us at Reader Service Preference Service, P.O. Box 9062, Buffalo, NY 14269. Include your complete name and address.

HSE11B

Angie Bartlett and Michael Robinson are friends. And following the death of his wife, Angie's best friend, their bond has grown even more. But that's all there is...right?

Read on for an exciting excerpt of WITHIN REACH by Sarah Mayberry, available August 2012 from Harlequin® Superromance®.

"HEY. RIGHT ON TIME," Michael said as he opened the door.

The first thing Angie registered was his fresh haircut and that he was clean shaven—a significant change from the last time she'd visited. Then her gaze dropped to his broad chest and the skintight black running pants molded to his muscular legs. The words died on her lips and she blinked, momentarily stunned by her acute awareness of him.

"You've cut your hair," she said stupidly.

"Yeah. Decided it was time to stop doing my caveman impersonation."

He gestured for her to enter. As she brushed past him she caught the scent of his spicy deodorant. He preceded her to the kitchen and her gaze traveled across his shoulders before dropping to his backside. Angie had always made a point of not noticing Michael's body. They were friends and she didn't want to know that kind of stuff. Now, however, she was forcibly reminded that he was a *very* attractive man.

Suddenly she didn't know where to look.

It was then that she noticed the other changes—the clean kitchen, the polished dining table and the living room free of clutter and abandoned clothes.

"Look at you go." Surely these efforts meant he was rejoining life.

He shrugged, but seemed pleased she'd noticed. "Getting there."

They maintained eye contact and the moment expanded. A connection that went beyond the boundaries of their friendship formed between them. Suddenly Angie wanted Michael in ways she'd never felt before. *Ever.*

"Okay. Let's get this show on the road," his six-year-old daughter, Eva, announced as she marched into the room.

Angie shook her head to break the spell and focused on Eva. "Great. Looking forward to a little light shopping?"

"Yes!" Eva gave a squeal of delight, then kissed her father goodbye.

Angie didn't feel 100 percent comfortable until she was sliding into the driver's seat.

Which was dumb. It was nothing. A stupid, odd bit of awareness that meant *nothing*. Michael was still Michael, even if he was gorgeous. Just because she'd tuned in to that fact for a few seconds didn't change anything.

Does Angie's new awareness mark a permanent shift in their relationship? Find out in WITHIN REACH by Sarah Mayberry, available August 2012 from Harlequin® Superromance®.

HSREXP0812

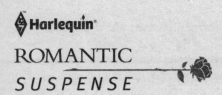

Harlequin

ROMANTIC

SUSPENSE

CINDY DEES

takes you on a wild journey to find the truth
in her new miniseries

Code X

Aiden McKay is more than just an ordinary man. As part of
an elite secret organization, Aiden was genetically enhanced
to increase his lung capacity and spend extended time under
water. He is a committed soldier, focused and dedicated
to his job. But when Aiden saves impulsive free spirit
Sunny Jordan from drowning she promptly overturns his
entire orderly, solitary world.

As the danger creeps closer, Adien soon realizes Sunny is the
target…but can he save her in time?

Breathless Encounter

Find out this August!

plus
**BONUS
STORY
INSIDE!**

Look out for a reader-favorite bonus story included in each
Harlequin Romantic Suspense book this August!

HARLEQUIN® HISTORICAL:
Where love is timeless

Fan-favorite author
JILLIAN HART
brings you a timeless tale of faith and love in

Montana Bride

Willa Conner learned a long time ago that love is a fairy tale.
She's been left widowed, pregnant and penniless, and her last
hope is the stranger who answers her ad for a husband.

Austin Dermot, a hardworking Montana blacksmith, doesn't
know what to expect from a mail-order bride. It certainly
isn't the brave, beautiful, but scarred young woman who
cautiously steps off the train....

Trust won't come easily for Willa—it's hard for her to believe
she's worthy of true love. But she doesn't need to worry about
that, because this is just a marriage of convenience...isn't it?

Can two strangers be a match made in the West?

Find out this August!